Baked With Love

The Boardwalk Bakery Romance

TINA MARTIN

~ * ~

ACKNOWLEDGEMENTS

This is title forty-four, YES, forty-four for me! Sometimes, I have a hard time believing it, too. LOL! While it's been a lot of hard work, it has also been an adventure because of you, my fantastic readers! I appreciate all the emails, the support on my social media sites and just the fact that you picked my book to read. Thank you for accepting my style of writing. I love you guys! A special thanks to my sister who reads every single book I write and calls me to talk about it like we're discussing a movie – you're awesome. Love ya, chick! Thanks to the fam who has to listen to me rant about these characters, but hey, characters are people, too! LOL.

Y'all keep reading and I'll keep writing.

Much love, Tina.

~ * ~

Dear Reader,

Welcome to the sweet world of Gianna Jacobsen. Gianna runs a little boardwalk bakery and life for her is mundane and somewhat normal. Then she meets Ramsey St. Claire and her boring little world of baking cupcakes is completely turned upside down. She's never had so much attention from a man, especially one like the incomparable, debonair Ramsey St. Claire. The man is everything. Yes, e-ve-ry-thing, and Gianna finds herself the *center* of his attention.

Gianna is a little *different*. Well, maybe more than a little. LOL! When I was writing her dialogue, I had to sit and laugh at certain points. She's that ditzy. But Ramsey must like 'em a lil' *cray-cray*. He's never met a woman like Gianna. She intrigues him. That's why after their not-so-ideal first encounter, he finds himself thinking about Gianna constantly. And he's intent on finding out why.

Enjoy this first part of *Baked With Love*. This is a three-part continuation series and perhaps the 'sweetest' love story you'll read all year. I know y'all hate continuation series. I've heard it all before (LOL) but these three will be back-to-back and you'll love it.

Happy reading, *cupcake*!

Tina

....

Welcome to The Boardwalk Bakery

::: Available Everyday :::
Vanilla Cupcakes (with white frosting and sprinkles)
Vanilla Cupcakes (with chocolate frosting and sprinkles)
Rich Chocolate, Devil's Food Cupcakes (with chocolate buttercream frosting)
Butter Pecan Cupcakes (with cream cheese frosting and pecan pieces)
Lemon (with lemon frosting)

::: Specialty Cupcakes :::
(Available on varying days of the week)

Banana Pudding
Cookies & Cream
Strawberry Shortcake
Red Velvet
Blueberry Lemon
Snickers

::: Drinks :::
Coffee (Small, Medium, Large)
Regular and Decaffeinated

We also cater! Call to place an order today!
704-555-BAKE

Visit us on Pinterest!

....

BAKED WITH LOVE
(The Boardwalk Bakery Romance)

PART ONE

Chapter 1

GIANNA REMOVED A fresh batch of vanilla cupcakes from the oven and placed them next to the others to cool in preparation for the next step – frosting. In the meantime, she slid in another batch. Lemon this time, her tenth batch of the morning.

"Shrew," she said as the oven's heat slapped her in the face. She closed the oven door and fanned flour dust away from her immediate space. It was a useless gesture. The kitchen in her bakery looked like flour-mageddon. A disaster. The equivalent of a man who couldn't cook tearing up his wife's kitchen. She grinned to herself thinking of how brutal men were in the kitchen – in anyone's kitchen – but today, she was no better than a non-cooking male. Her black apron was covered with the dusty, white stuff as well as her black, no-slip, off-brand shoes. And why on earth did she buy black aprons over white ones? She couldn't recall a specific reason. Maybe they were on sale or something. Most likely, that was the reason. With her budget, all she could afford was sale items. Whatever the case, black aprons in a bakery just didn't make much sense. Maybe in some upscale, fancy restaurant, but definitely not a bakery. At least not *her* bakery.

Gianna coughed. Fanning, again. The Boardwalk Bakery – with its pastel pink walls and ten black, tables with four chairs to each – didn't see much action in the mornings. It wasn't until noon that the place started jumping with customers looking to fulfill their cravings for early afternoon sugar – something to help them make it through the rest of the day on their stuffy, corporate jobs. Gianna was accustomed to the routine. It gave her time in the mornings to prepare for the midday rush, especially since the early risers who wandered through her doors only wanted coffee. Did people *not* eat cupcakes in the morning? Probably not since they were considered a dessert and not morning breakfast pastries. With that being the case why was she consistently opening at 9:00 a.m.? Just to sell ten cups of coffee? It was hardly worth the effort.

Maybe I should only open in the afternoons, she considered, chewing on her bottom lip as she did so. But that still meant she'd have to come to the bakery early to prepare, so—

When her cell phone rang, she ran to the back office – the only office in the bakery – to retrieve it, recognizing her sister Gemma's upbeat ringtone. Gemma was the only contact in her phone with an assigned ringtone. That was one way to ensure that she'd never miss a call from Gemma.

"Hey, Gem. I've been waiting for your call. How'd it go?" Gianna asked, heaving. Coughing.

"Gianna, why do you sound like you're out of breath?" Gemma asked.

"Because I *am* out of breath. When I heard the phone, I ran to the office to get it. Plus, there's so much flour floating around in the air, I feel like I'm trapped in a snow globe. It's all up in my lungs," she said, fanning.

"Why don't you crack open a door or something?"

Gianna chuckled. "It's flour, Gemma. Not smoke."

"Laugh now, die of flour inhalation later."

Gianna laughed again. "Anyway, silly, tell me how it went. Was it bad?"

"No. Well, it's bad that I have to get chemo, but—" Gemma blew a breath. "I just hope it works. I want to be around to bug you for a very long time."

"And I want you to bug me," Gianna said with the cell phone pinched between her left ear and shoulder while she carried a tray of her best-selling butter pecan cupcakes to the front. She would put them in the display case when she got off the phone.

Leaning against the counter with her back towards the entrance, she crossed her legs at the ankles and held the phone with her left hand again. "So, you can't give me any more details about the procedure?"

"No, and we don't have to talk about cancer every time we speak, Gianna."

"I know. I know. I'm just concerned. That's all. Can't I be concerned for my *whittle* sister?"

"Oh, jeez," Gemma said. "Not the baby talk."

"Can't I?" Gianna asked again, this time dropping the *whittle*, but still amused by it.

"You can, but be adult-concerned. You're all, goo-goo ga-ga, concerned. If I was there, you'd pinch my cheeks, wouldn't you?"

Doing her best baby talk impression, Gianna said, "I sure would pinch those chubby *whittle* cheeks of yours."

The sound of a man clearing his throat made Gianna spin around quickly to see who it was that had apparently snuck up in her shop. Snuck up on her. Her heart drummed in her chest when her eyes beheld the tall, six-foot-something of a man clad in a black suit standing there.

"Oh my God!" she screamed, throwing her right hand over her chest like the gesture would help to soothe her pounding heart. "You scared the crap out of me!"

With a deep, sophisticated voice, he said, "I was standing here, waiting for you to turn around. I apologize if—"

She threw up a twitchy index finger. "Hold that thought."

She turned around again, back facing him and returned her attention to her phone.

"Hello?" she said to make sure Gemma was still on the line.

"I'm here. What's wrong, Gianna?" Gemma asked. "I heard you scream."

"Gemma, I'll call you later. I have to go."

"What's wrong?"

Gianna glanced back at the man again, feeling her breaths quicken. Men always made her uneasy especially since she didn't have much experience with them. Honestly, she didn't have any experience with them. And this one in particular – sweet mercy. He looked milk chocolate, like the icing she was going to put on her Devil's food cupcakes.

Returning her attention to the phone again, she whispered to Gemma, "There's a giant of a man in here and he looks hungry—no, not hungry. *Hangry*...a combination of hungry and angry."

The man frowned slightly and smirked. Did she really think she was whispering?

"Ooh," Gemma replied. "Is he *hangry* and cute?"

"Gem, I have to go."

"Just answer the question, Gianna."

"Okay, yes. He's cute, now I have to go."

"Wait, wait, wait...how tall is he?"

"What does that matter?"

"Ugh...just tell me."

Gianna turned around again, her eyes doing a full sweep of the distinguished gentleman. Then she told her sister, "Yes, he's tall. He's so tall, his head will touch the ceiling if he jumps."

The man looked up at the ceiling, cracked a

half smile and shook his head. This was actually happening. What kind of bakery had he walked into?

Gemma laughed. "He ain't *that* tall, Gianna."

"Well, he's tall enough to make me feel short."

"That's because you *are* short, shorty," Gemma quipped.

"Okay, I gotta go, sis. This guy's getting antsy."

"Alright," Gemma said. "Talk to you later."

"Love ya. Bye." Gianna slid her phone into one of the pockets on her dusty apron, looked at the gentleman and with her eyes narrowed to slits, she asked, "What the *freak* was that about?"

"Excuse me?" he asked, amused.

"You snuck up on me."

"I did no such thing," he said, his voice smooth and deep. "I *walked* into a place of business."

Gianna felt a wave of heat rush through her body. The pure gorgeousness of this man had instantly given her hot flashes – those big ol' broad shoulders on a lean body, lips that looked like they'd latch right on to anything and eyes darker than his suit. He was clean shaven. Mustache trimmed. Haircut fresh and neat. The base notes of his cologne snatched the smell of cupcakes right out of her nose.

She got ahold of herself, somewhat, crossed her arms over chest and said, "Well, I didn't hear the bell ding-a-ling."

He grinned. "You didn't..." He laughed

harder and could hardly get the rest of the question out. "You didn't hear the bell do what?"

"Ding-a-ling." She cleared her throat, not that it needed to be cleared. "That's why I...why I said you snuck up on me. Anyway, what can I get you?"

He gazed at her for a moment about to explode with more laughter.

Gianna frowned. *Why is he smiling? What's wrong with this guy? Ask him why he's smiling. Ask him! No, don't ask him. Don't...*

"Why are you smiling?" she asked deciding to find out, going against her better judgment.

His smile turned into a light chuckle.

Narrowing her eyes, she asked, "Are you laughing at me?"

"Yes, I am and, by the way, you have something white on the tip of your nose. I'm assuming it's flour. Well, I *hope* it's flour. Here, allow me." He reached out and wiped the substance from her nose using the back of his index finger.

At his touch, her entire body shook – not trembled – but actually jerked and wiggled like those twenty-feet tall, inflatable air dancers in front of a car dealership. Her legs went so weak, she had to catch herself from falling by placing her hands flat on the counter. The man must've thought she was nuts but in her defense, she'd never been touched by a man before, innocent or otherwise. And she'd never been in the presence of *this* kind of man – the kind of man you can look at and instantly tell

13

he was somebody important. The kind of man that rocked five-thousand dollar, tailored suits. The kind of man who had the boldness to wipe something off of a woman's nose without waiting for permission to do so because he knew he could get away with it. He could get away with anything with his fine behind.

"Are you okay?" he asked.

"Lips," she replied.

He looked confused. *Okay, so maybe that wasn't flour on her nose. This woman is weird.* "Come again?"

"I'm sorry," she said blinking profusely and shaking her head like she had to physically juggle her brain around to regain focus. "What did you ask me?"

Amused, he released a small chuckle before he responded, "I asked you if you were okay, but never mind. You've pretty much answered my question already."

Her eyes narrowed even further when she replied, "You think I'm a fruitcake don't you?"

He frowned and quirked his mouth into a lopsided grin.

"Well, I got news for you, buddy. I'm not fruitcake. I can assure you. I don't even like fruitcake."

"Nobody likes fruitcake," he said. "Why are you so nervous right now?"

Why are you so ferociously male, taking over my little bakery with your testosterone and distinctive spellbinding scent? Hunh? Answer that, buster!

"Hello?" he said, making a waving motion

with his hand to get her attention. She had to have been the strangest woman he'd ever encountered. "Are you high right now?"

High off of your cologne. Yep. "No, I'm not high! I am a little freaked out because you *snuck* up on me."

"I didn't sneak up on you. Okay. This is a place of business. I came inside. Why are you so nervous?"

"You already asked me that."

"And I'm still waiting for an answer."

"You know what," she said, then giggled. The out of place laughter made her look even more nervous and panicky. "Let's just cut the small talk or whatever this is. I'm sure you have somewhere important to be, so what can I get for you?"

"I want a cupcake."

"What!" she screeched.

He frowned. Okay, this confirmed it for him. Something was really wrong with this chick. "This *is* a specialty cupcake bakery isn't it?"

"Yes, but—"

"Then why are you yelling like I just pulled a gun out on you?" he interrupted her to ask. "I *did* just order a cupcake. Am I ordering incorrectly, or what? Do you have some special cupcake ordering system that I'm not privy to?"

She glared at him. "No, but you *are* ordering incorrectly and you know exactly what you're doing...playing around with words."

He was beside himself. "Look, lady, I simply said I wanted to order a cupcake."

"No. You said you want *my* cupcake."

He erupted in laughter. "No. I said I want *a* cupcake."

Gianna crossed her arms again, staring at the man and his beautiful white smile. "I know what I heard."

"And I know what I said," he countered. "Now, can I get one of those butter pecan cupcakes, or are you holding them hostage?"

"Okay. Fine. One *butter* pecan coming right up," she said unenthused. She slid a clear, plastic serving glove on her right hand, then took one of the freshly baked butter pecan cupcakes from the tray on the counter. She never did get around to putting them in the display case.

Glancing at him as he looked around the bakery, she asked, "Is this for here or to go?" *Please say to go. Please say to go.*

He had planned on taking it to go, along with a coffee, but now that he'd been thoroughly entertained by her, he wanted to stick around for more of her antics. "For here, please."

Eyebrows raised, she asked, "You—you said, for here?"

He could sense she hadn't expected him to dine in. "Yes. For here. Do I need to dust flour out of your ears, too?"

She smiled. "Sorry. I heard you."

"You're smiling. Does that mean you're normal?"

"Somewhat," she responded. "I'm just a little rattled."

"A *little*?" His lips formed into a sensuous

smile. "How about a lot? You've been high-strung since you realized I was here."

"I know. I know. It's no excuse, but I don't usually get people in here this early in the mornings."

"But when you do, you tell your sister how cute and tall they are."

Gianna's mouth fell open in shock.

"Newsflash, cupcake lady...you can't whisper worth a lick," the man informed her.

He watched as her already reddened cheeks turned a shade darker with embarrassment.

"To your point, though, I *am* cute and tall, although I would prefer *handsome* over cute. Remember that the next time you're describing me to your sister."

Gianna could only shake her head. "First of all, how did you know I was talking to my sister?"

"You mean your *whittle* sister?" He laughed.

She felt like locking herself in her office until he left. That's how utterly embarrassed she was. Changing the subject, she asked, "Would you like some coffee?"

"I would like some coffee."

"Small, medium or large?"

He smirked. "What do you think?"

She looked up at him. "Right. Large."

He nodded.

She bent down to take a large paper cup from the shelf then placed it on the counter. "The sleeves and tops are over there by the cream, sugar and the...um...the..."

"Coffee?"

"Yes. The coffee," she said smiling nervously, glancing at him then quickly returning her attention back to the cash register. After pressing a few more keys, she said, "And your total comes to $6.18."

He pulled out his wallet from the back right pocket of his pants and took out a twenty-dollar bill, handing it to her. Before Gianna could give him change, he said, "Put the change in your tip jar."

"I don't have a tip jar."

"You should. Your pocket will suffice for now."

"Um...okay. Thank you for the tip."

"Thank you for the cupcake and coffee. Finally." He smiled again, then took the cupcake and cup from the counter, heading for the coffee station. After preparing his coffee until the color of it matched the woman's skin tone – smooth and buttery brown – he sat where he would have a good view of her. He'd never met a more fidgety, uneasy woman. Granted, most women found themselves unnerved around him. That's just the kind of hair-raising effect he had on women. And he could easily distinguish between the ones he could readily have and the women who would prove to be more of a challenge.

This woman, however, had him off his game. He couldn't quite read her just yet, but he knew one thing for sure – she made some delicious, mouthwatering cupcakes. And everything about her appearance was beautiful in an innocent kind of way. He couldn't see her hair because of the hairnet she was wearing, but he could tell it was black and balled up into a bun. Her skin complexion was a few shades lighter than his. She looked to be about five and a half feet tall. She didn't have a curvy body from what he could see. She looked thin – straight up and down. And she had to be a smart woman. A little flaky, but smart. It took guts to run a small business, especially a niche market like specialty cupcakes where the profit margin was low and operating costs were high. He wondered how long she'd been in business, and if she ran the bakery alone.

He took a sip of coffee then removed his cell phone from his suit jacket. After pulling up a web browser, he Googled her bakery name – The Boardwalk Bakery – just to satisfy his curiosity on whether or not the bakery had an online presence. It hadn't. And his search results yielded no reviews. No social media sites. Just a few listings showing the business name, number and address.

He glanced up when he felt her eyes on him and as soon as he met her light brown gaze, she looked away, continuing to wipe the counter in counterclockwise circles.

He took a sip of coffee, analyzing her – his eyes traveling down to her legs then back up to her oval shaped face. If he was correct in reading her, she looked like she wanted to ask him something but was hesitant to do so. That didn't surprise him. Her hesitancy that is. He'd been told a time or two (truthfully speaking, more like a hundred times) that his presence was intimidating. Besides, the cupcake lady didn't come off as a conversationalist and that had him guessing her age. Mid-twenties? Late twenties? There was no way she was a day over thirty.

His thoughts were interrupted by a tinkling bell at the entrance. He grinned to himself. *So, there is a doorbell. Why didn't it tinkle when I came in?*

He shifted his body to take a look at the door. There wasn't an electric chime doorbell, but an actual bell hanging from the interior side of the door. Apparently, it was faulty because it certainly didn't tinkle twenty minutes ago.

Putting the doorbell concern on hold for the moment, he sat up tall watching a man who appeared to be homeless walk in – not that he was being judgy, but what else was he supposed to think by the appearance of the man? He looked like he hadn't shaved in months and wore a dirty white T-shirt and worn, black shoes. He'd never seen a once-white T-shirt so filthy. And the khaki cargo pants the man wore had seen many bad days.

He watched the woman emerge from the kitchen and witnessed the moment her eyes lit up when she saw the homeless man.

"Hey, Jerry!" he said.

"Good *moanin'* sweet thang. I see you done got yaself a customer dis moanin'."

"Something like that," Gianna said glancing over at the well-dressed gentleman who'd nearly frightened her half to death. He was looking back at her. She looked away from him, returning her attention to Jerry again. "I got something good for you. Be right back."

She went to the kitchen for a moment, grabbed a box of cupcakes and, back at the front, she placed it on the counter. "Here you go. These were especially made with love for one of my fa-vo-rite people. You have three buttercream chocolate and three cream cheese carrot cupcakes."

"Sounds good to me," he said, rubbing his stomach. "Bless you, sweet thang." He took the box and headed for the door.

"Have a good day, Jerry."

"I will thanks to you."

She smiled, satisfied she was able to do something to brighten Jerry's day. "Don't forget to share."

"Yes, ma'am," Jerry said immediately before he exited.

Still smiling, Gianna glanced over at the suited-up man who'd unnerved her and interrupted her morning, feeling the smile instantly fall away from her face. Why was he staring so hard?

And he continued staring with his large hand wrapped around the tall coffee cup, sipping and reflecting on her interaction with the homeless man. He was on alert when the man came in, but it was obvious she knew who this guy was. And she'd given him a box of cupcakes for free. It only piqued his curiosity about cupcake lady. Exactly who was this woman?

Chapter 2

RAMSEY ST. CLAIRE sat behind his exquisite, smoked pecan executive desk waiting for his project managers to show up. On the agenda – the new two-hundred-unit apartment complex to be constructed in the up and coming Belgate Community located in the University City area of North Charlotte. With the nearly completed construction of the new light rail tracks running through the center of the inbound and outbound lanes of North Tryon Street, providing a crucial connection between the university area (UNC-Charlotte) and Uptown, the surrounding land was a hot seller for developers and was being snatched up on a first come, first served basis as long as you had the capital. And St. Claire Architects had millions at their disposal. Since a part of the firm's appeal was the extra step they took to find land for developers in addition to designing their structures, they stood to make millions once the project was finalized.

"Gentlemen, good morning," Ramsey said, sitting up in his chair as his project managers – Ralph Sheppard and Gilbert Lewis walked into his office with tablets in their hand.

"Good morning, Ram," Ralph said. "What's

going on?"

"Yeah, man. You never call meetings this early in the morning," Gilbert said.

"I don't usually, but I need a progress report on the U-City project ASAP."

"We're still in phase one as you're aware," Ralph said.

Ramsey leaned back in his chair hiding a grimace. He prided himself on the ability to keep a cool head under pressure or when he was irritated. At the moment he was irritated. Phase one should have been completed a week ago. Ramsey didn't like setbacks of any kind. When projects weren't completed, on time, it only put them, as a company, further behind, thus delaying other projects they could acquire. Instead of taking on another assignment, they were *stuck* on phase one. He didn't make his millions off of delays and being stuck in phase one. He made his money getting stuff done and on time. He didn't like his bank account being toyed with because people wanted to be lazy.

Ramsey sat up in his chair again. "I was at the University City site today. Imagine my surprise to see that the land has yet to be completely excavated."

"There's an explanation for that," Gilbert said quickly, just about cutting him off.

"Then I would like to hear it."

"The excavation company we went with backed out before the job was complete," he explained.

"When did this happen?" Ramsey asked frowning. It certainly was news to him.

"Two weeks ago."

"Did you notify Royal?" His younger brother, Royal, was the troubleshooter for St. Claire Architects and was to be informed of all project delays.

"Yes," Gilbert answered. "Royal was notified the same day of the walkout."

Strange, because Ramsey didn't recall Royal mentioning this in any of their status meetings.

"So, two whole weeks, fourteen days, the land is just sitting there, screaming for help and what do we do about it? Nothing but fold our hands." Ramsey brought his hands to a steeple. "Why am I just hearing about this now, fellas?" he asked because even though Royal was the troubleshooter and the person he *should've* gotten this update from, the project managers still had an obligation to notify Ramsey of any urgent issues that needed attention.

"It's my fault," Gilbert admitted. "I was hoping to get the situation handled without having to involve you. I know how busy you are, Sir."

"Then, since you chose to leave me out of it, what have you been doing to get the problem resolved?"

"We found a new excavation group," Ralph jumped in to say, so Gilbert didn't take all the heat.

"Which one?"

"McFarlane."

"McFarlane." The name jogged Ramsey's memory. "Isn't that the group working on those new Ikea Boulevard apartments?"

Ralph nodded. "Yes, I believe it is."

"With that big of an undertaking, do they have the manpower to start our project?"

"The owner assured me that they did, Sir."

"And when are they starting?" Ramsey asked. "Please say tomorrow."

"We tried to get them as soon as we could. The earliest they can start is Monday," Gilbert said.

Monday? A muscle twitched in Ramsey's jaw. Today was Wednesday, and they had to wait until Monday? He didn't like that one bit. That meant that all day today, Thursday, Friday, Saturday and Sunday was wasted time – time that could've been spent clearing the property had they hired the right company the first time around.

"You gave us a little leeway with this project, Ram," Gilbert said. "Why the sudden urgency?"

Ramsey exhaled an even sigh, propping his head up with his left hand, using his thumb to massage his temple. Gilbert had some nerve asking him a question like that, but the man was right. He *did* give the project managers flexibility on the University City project. Normally, he'd be in grind mode – the usual for him, but not this time. Why? Because he was burnt out, not really feeling the routine of doing the same job day in and day out. Granted, he loved architecture, especially the aesthetics side of it, and his firm was featured in numerous magazines – *Architectural Digest*, *Metropolis*, *The Blueprint*, *Wallpaper* and

BuildIt – but he needed a break from it all. His brothers had been trying to convince him for the last year that he deserved to take some time off. He finally listened. But did his decision to take a break mean that nothing was going to get done while he was gone? That projects would fail to meet target dates and contractors could take their sweet time doing their part of the construction? He couldn't have that. He needed assurances. Needed to be in control, even if he did take a hiatus from work.

Deciding to level with his project managers, he said, "I've been thinking about taking some time off. I wanted to see some progress on this project before I left."

Ralph sat straight up in his chair when he asked, "You're taking time off?"

Gilbert appeared to be just as shocked as Ralph.

"Yes. I'm considering it," Ramsey said.

Gilbert's brows almost touched as his mind tried to process this anomaly of Ramsey St. Claire taking time off work. "But you never take time off."

"And that's precisely why I'm seriously considering it. If I follow through, I will be gone one-hundred percent of the time and the only exception would be coming to the office for extreme emergencies. Otherwise, I'll be checking my emails regularly from home in case Judy has something for me to approve. Now, it's paramount that we get this land cleared, and since you said McFarlane will be starting on Monday, I'll be there to make sure they do."

"They will," Ralph said. "I'm sure of it."

"Do I need to interfere to get the ball rolling on this?" Ramsey asked, eyeing them skeptically. It was a bad feeling to lose faith in his project managers but that's where Ramsey found himself currently.

"No, Ram," Ralph answered. "We can take care of this. We *are* taking care of this. You deserve a break. You relax. Let us do the worrying."

"When you own your own business, Ralph, all you do is worry, hope for the best but expect the worst. On Monday, I'm hoping for the best. I'm not expecting the worst and if the worst happens, somebody's job will be in jeopardy. Are we clear?"

"Yes, Sir," Ralph said.

"Clear as glass, Sir," Gilbert responded.

"Is there anything else either of you needs to discuss with me?"

"No," Gilbert said.

Ralph shook his head.

"Then you can return to your duties. Thank you for your time."

After dismissing the men, Ramsey hit the speakerphone button on his phone and punched in Royal's extension.

Royal's voice came through the speaker. "Sup, Ram?"

"I just met with Ralph and Gilbert."

"Okay."

"They said they updated you on the excavation delay with the University City project."

"They did."

Ramsey balled his hands into fists. The joys of working with family members...

He knew the personal relationships he had with his brothers could make professional relationships with them that much more difficult, but they had the knowledge and expertise to do their individual jobs – even Royal who'd just graduated from college last year with a degree in business analytics. His problem with Royal was his attitude – he'd been dubbed the *cool* St. Claire around the office – the one people felt most comfortable talking to because the rest of them were supposedly short-tempered, strict and by-the-book. Royal was developing the habit of letting things slide. Giving people second, third and fourth chances. Hanging on to employees that should've been fired. He caused problems instead of troubleshooting them. He was more laid back and relaxed – too laid back as far as Ramsey was concerned.

"Royal, why didn't you make me aware of this at our last status meeting?"

"Because we're operating three months ahead of schedule on this project. Plus, I didn't want you getting all wound up for nothing. You're already burnt out."

"I'm not burnt out—"

"You are, walking around here like you're mad at the world. Everybody sees how cranky you are. Well, everyone besides you."

"Even if that was true, it still doesn't justify

your negligence when it comes to notifying me about crucial project delays, man. It's your job, Roy!"

"I know what my job entails."

"Then I expect you to do it, or you're going to find yourself without one." Ramsey pressed the speakerphone button to end the call.

He stood up, blew a breath and stood in front of the floor-to-ceiling windows of his tenth floor, lavish office – decorated with tall, leafy tropical plants, several tranquil fountains and a wet bar. He could stand a drink at the moment but chose to go without one for now. Royal was partially right. He was easily irritable as of late – frustrated with trivial matters at the firm and forging ahead with projects that weren't late or close to being overdue. He wasn't a jerk. Nowhere close to being a jerk. So why had he been acting like one?

Ramsey leaned against a window and closed his eyes searching for something to calm his temper and that's when he thought of her – cupcake lady. It was in this moment he realized he didn't know the woman's name. What he *did* know was he liked her quirky and skittish ways. She was funny, and he didn't think it was intentional which made her behavior even more amusing. She was being her natural self. He smiled to himself when he pictured flour on the tip of her nose. He chuckled at the way she screamed when she realized he was standing behind her. And, as he consumed what he considered to be the best cupcake he'd ever eaten, he watched her work behind the counter, adding cupcakes to the display case and tidying up the place. Then there was the man who came into the bakery. The homeless fella. She'd given him a box of cupcakes. Who was he exactly?

His thoughts were interrupted too soon by his secretary's voice emitting through his phone's intercom saying, "Mr. St. Claire, there's a Felicity James on the line for you, Sir. Should I put her through?"

He walked over to his desk, pressed the intercom button and said, "Yes, send it through, Judy."

"Coming your way," she responded.

Great. Now he had to deal with this convoluted mess, and he couldn't blame anyone but himself. He released a deep sigh and tapped his knuckles on his wooden desk. Four weeks ago, he'd contacted Felicity James of Wedded Bliss, Inc. – the first of its kind matchmaking service in Charlotte catered to helping men. Wedded Bliss specialized in finding wives for busy, high-ranking businessmen who either didn't have time to date or who chose not to go through all the rigmarole to find a suitable trophy wife. They were too busy running their businesses or advancing their careers to spend an undetermined amount of time searching for Mrs. Right. Still, they needed one. Seemed people felt comfortable doing business with a man who could show that he could be a businessman and family man all rolled up into one extraordinary human.

That's where Felicity came in. After the men completed a thorough, ten-page profile of themselves, in addition to writing a description of their perfect woman, Felicity would carefully choose three women from her database who she deemed as matches. She'd sent Ramsey three matches a month ago and had yet to hear from him.

"Ms. James, how goes it?" he asked.

"I'm doing well, Mr. St. Claire. How about yourself?"

"I'm good. And busy. Good and busy." He managed a grin.

"You must be. When I didn't hear from you, I thought you were out of the country again."

When she had contacted him the week after emailing the three profiles, he *was* out of the country – in Paris with his brother Regal. Even though that was the case, he still could've studied the profiles, but he hadn't bothered. On one end, he liked the convenience of the services Wedded Bliss offered, but on the other, finding a wife, a partner in life partner should've been more personal than going to a matchmaking service. But that's precisely why he went. He'd been in love once in his lifetime. One time, and he had no desire, no yearning – nothing in him wanted to fall in love again. He just wanted a wife because he felt like he had to have one. A companion. Someone to bounce his thoughts and ideas off of. Someone to satisfy his mother's constant nagging about her oldest son settling down and becoming an example for his brothers. Wedded Bliss provided the fastest way for him to accomplish that.

"I'm not out of the country, Mrs. James. I'm here. I've just been busy."

"Okay, umm...I'm picking up a different vibe here," Felicity said. "You don't want to go through this, do you?"

"*I do*...no pun intended." He chuckled.

"Well, have you looked at the profiles?"

"No. I honestly didn't have time to."

"Four weeks and not even a peek?"

"No. I run *the* most successful architecture firm in Charlotte. My time is very limited."

"You knew that before you hired me, did you not?"

She had him there. "I did. Yes. Okay. I will make it a point today to print out the profiles and go over them with a fine-tooth comb. You know how particular I am."

"Yes, I do, which is why I chose the best of the best for you. Your future wife is in your inbox, Mr. St. Claire. You just have to take the initiative and open the email first."

He laughed. *Your wife is in your inbox.* "Okay. I'll have a look."

"Today?"

"Yes. Today."

"Okay, but just so I know you're serious this time, I'm going to need you to come by my office tomorrow afternoon, let's say around four to go over those profiles. So print—"

"Sorry to interrupt you Ms. James, but I do not have the time to drive to South Park tomorrow. I don't see why we can't do this over the phone."

"Because I need to know that you're committed to this process, and as it stands, I don't feel like you're taking this seriously. You're already beyond the thirty days on this and it's your own fault, Mr. St. Claire. If you're not here tomorrow, unfortunately, I'll have to place you as inactive in our database which will also mean, you forfeit your five-thousand dollar deposit."

Ramsey groaned. He could not care less about the five grand even if he did want to drop out of the service, which he didn't. He needed a wife – one whom he could lay out some ground rules and she'd oblige without much resistance or expectations. "Okay. Tomorrow. Four o'clock. Got it."

"Wonderful. Have a good day, Mr. St. Claire."

"You as well."

He hung up the phone and rubbed his forehead. *I should've never signed up for this.* Then he thought about what Felicity had said – your wife is in your inbox. So, he found her email, opened the three attachments and immediately printed them out. The profiles had the women's first names, a single photo and descriptions of them:

Name: Irma Lakes
Age: 26
Occupation: Dental Assistant

Description: Hi. I'm Irma! I'm a family oriented gal who loves to fish, sing, dance and have fun. Any time with me is a good time.

———————

Ramsey rolled his eyes. "You can have fun with somebody else, gal," he mumbled. He went on to the second one:

Name: Cayla Cartwright
Age: 31
Occupation: IT Consultant
Description: I'm too busy to date, so I decided this was the best route for me to find the perfect man to be my husband. I'm looking for Mr. Tall, Dark and Extremely Handsome who's good with his hands and wants kids. I don't ask for much, just be who you say you are and we'll be just fine.

———————

Ramsey sighed heavily. There was no way he'd give Cayla Cartwright any consideration simply because of the emphasis she placed on her ideal man's physical appearance – tall, dark and *extremely* handsome. Seemed she cared about the man's looks more than who he was as a person. He went on to the last profile:

Name: Shelly Langford
Age: 28
Occupation: Middle Math School Teacher

Description: Hello. I'm good at Math. Meeting people, not so much. I like to entertain and looking for someone who loves to travel, who's good with people and can hold a conversation.

———————

Frustrated, Ramsey dropped the profiles on his desk and returned to the windows, staring down at the pond below – one he'd designed eight years ago before the doors of St. Claire Architects opened. The women Felicity chose for him were pretty, and maybe they were interesting to some other man, but not him. That's when he realized that signing up for this service was a bad idea, and he would tell Felicity that in person tomorrow. None of these women didn't sound half as interesting as the woman he'd met today – whatever her name was. Tomorrow, he'd make it his mission to find out.

Chapter 3

AFTER LOCKING UP the bakery, Gianna rushed home to her three-bedroom house, eager to see her sister since, today, Gemma had gotten her first chemotherapy treatment. If she didn't have to open the bakery, she would've been right there at the hospital with her. But she had to work. It was the only income to support herself and her sister.

As soon as she unlocked the door, she called out, "Gemma, where are you?"

"In here," was Gemma's groggy, unenthusiastic reply.

Gianna rounded the corner, took a few steps down the small hallway and immediately saw her sister's pale, freckled face as she laid in bed. Since she was getting chemo, Gemma decided to cut her hair short so she wouldn't feel so bad about it falling out. The little she had left was standing straight up in the air like it hadn't seen a brush all day. It probably hadn't. Gemma usually kept her hair hidden beneath a scarf. Right now, she looked like she could barely keep her eyes open.

Standing beside the bed, Gianna asked, "Why is it so hot in here, Gem? You didn't turn the air on?"

"No. It feels fine in here."

"No, it doesn't feel fine. It's hot and stuffy." She touched her sister's forehead with the backside of her hand. "You have a slight temperature, and you look a mess, Gem."

"Well, I feel a mess, so there," she drawled.

Gianna helped her sit up and made her comfortable by adjusting the pillows behind her back. "Have you eaten?"

"Why? So I can throw it all back up again? No thanks."

"Gem, you have to eat something. Let me go see what we have."

"Good luck with that. The fridge is as empty as my hopes and dreams."

"Come on, Gem. Don't kid around like that."

Gemma shrugged. "I'm just sayin'."

Gianna sighed heavily, looking at her sister. She knew she was joking, but her words actually stung. She wanted so much more for her sister. She didn't deserve this. "Let me go see what we have. I'll be right back."

Gianna walked to the kitchen, opened the refrigerator to see that it was bare.

"Jeez," she said in an undertone, pushing the refrigerator door shut. Then she walked over to the pantry, discovering they were also out of soup, Gemma's food of choice – pretty much the only food guaranteed not to give her heartburn and was simple to eat. She grumbled while her stomach rumbled. "Now, I need to leave her alone yet *again* to pick up some food."

Gianna felt bad enough that she couldn't go

to her sister's appointment today. Now, she couldn't even cook her anything to eat. She nibbled on her bottom lip.

Okay...think, Gianna. You could just run to a grocery store. It's only a few miles from here. Gemma will be okay until you get back. But what if she wasn't okay? What if she passed out or slipped and hit her head while trying to walk to the bathroom or something? What then?

Leaning against the counter in the kitchen, Gianna held her head and attempted a deep breathing technique – something her doctor told her to do whenever she felt like she was under too much pressure. Lately, she'd been feeling it a lot, but it wasn't nearly as bad as the first time she started having anxiety attacks – when she found out her little sister had cancer. She'd passed out then, right there in the doctor's office. She couldn't pass out now. Gemma needed her to be strong.

She pulled one long breath in and released a long breath out.

"Think, Gianna. Think."

Long breath in...

Then the doorbell rang and snapped her out of her breathing technique because she remembered that her best friend, Felicity was coming over today.

Felicity!

Why didn't it dawn on her to call Felicity and have her bring some food? She rushed to the front door as the doorbell sounded again and when she opened it, there stood Felicity holding two takeout bags.

"You read my mind. Thank you!" Gianna said, hugging her friend.

"Gianna, why are you choking me, girlfriend?"

"Because I was freaking out, on the verge of another anxiety attack when I realized I didn't have any food in this house and I was afraid to leave Gemma home to go get something. Then you showed up! You're a lifesaver. Thank you!"

"Okay, anaconda, let me go so I can breathe."

"Oh, sorry. Okay. Come in."

"Thank you," Felicity said, stepping inside. "I *did* tell you I was coming over today, didn't I? I'm sure I did."

"Yes, you did. I just forgot. It's been such a hectic day at the bakery and—"

"Gianna, calm down. You sound all panicky. Ew. I don't want that rubbing off on me. Sit down, girl. Take a breath."

"Right," Gianna agreed, pacing her breaths.

In the kitchen, Felicity stepped out of her heels then took a container of rice out of the bag. "I got this for Gemma. Do you think she can eat that?"

"Yes, but I don't know if she's up to eating."

"I'll give it to her, anyway," Felicity said. "Be right back."

While she was gone, Gianna opened her takeout box to reveal sesame chicken with fried rice. She began eating, nearly inhaling the food. "This is so good," she mumbled.

"Did you not eat at all this week?" Felicity

quipped, walking into the kitchen.

"You know I rarely take lunch breaks. I mean, how can I? Cupcakes have to be baked and frosted."

"I understand that, but you have to eat," Felicity said, taking a seat, starting on her dinner.

"Well, I wasn't hungry at work, but now I'm starving."

"I can see that," Felicity said.

"Was Gemma awake?" Gianna asked.

"Barely, although I think the smell of that fried rice got her eyes open. She's probably eating it now." Felicity stirred her rice. "So, did she talk to you about the treatment?"

"She did, but she was very vague about it. She hasn't been exactly forthcoming with information these days. She just said the treatment made her feel sick."

"Does she know that Dr. Willoughby told you she had...um...roughly two months to live if the chemo doesn't work?"

Gianna shook her head slowly. "She doesn't know that I know. I just pray that it works. Dr. Willoughby told me to be optimistic." Gianna tried to take the doctor's advice, but with a mounting pile of medical bills and no assurances from the doctors that Gemma had a real chance, she found herself more pessimistic, anxious and nervy than anything else.

"I'm praying for her, Gianna, and you."

Gianna smiled warmly at her friend. When they were growing up together, Felicity was always the feisty, loud-mouthed, outgoing one. The cheerleader. The kind of girl who could get any man she wanted. Who could *do* anything she wanted. That's why they made good friends – they were exact opposites – and even though that was the case, Felicity had always been a loyal friend. "Thank you, Felicity. And thanks for bringing food."

"You're welcome, as always." Felicity took a drink of water. "Since your day was hectic, I take it business must be picking up now, huh?"

"Well, no. Not really."

"Then what happened today?"

Gianna smiled. "Nothing." She shook her head, remembering how much of a fool she'd made of herself. She'd never been comfortable around men—especially good-looking, accomplished, confident ones who *knew* they had it like that. And the guy who stopped by her bakery today definitely had it like that.

Felicity's eyes narrowed. "You're holding back. Tell me what happened?"

"It's just that this guy came in this morning and sort of threw my whole day off balance."

Felicity stopped chewing. "What guy?"

"I don't know. Tall. Black. Gorgeous. And he smelled so dang good, Felicity. I can still smell him and just his scent alone had me trembling in my shoes."

Felicity chuckled. "Don't tell me he had you all flustered..."

Gianna grinned.

"Oh, gosh. He had you all flustered," Felicity said. "How many times have I told you to never let a man see how much you like him?"

"It wasn't that I liked him. I was just nervous."

She raised a brow. "Nervous?"

"Felicity, you know me. I'm a nervous wreck without having to be around a hot guy, so you can about imagine how nervous I was in the presence of one. I couldn't think straight—had a hard time focusing. At one point, I got hot flashes...thought I was going to faint."

Felicity chuckled. "You're too funny. Ain't no man gonna have me shook to the point that I feel like I'm going to faint."

"Yes, because you're you. You've always been super confident. Me, on the other hand—I try to avoid men as much as possible so they don't find out how weird I am. But this guy I couldn't avoid. He was standing at the counter, staring at me...playing games with my head."

"What?" Felicity laughed.

"He was playing games with me."

Felicity quirked up her lips. "How was he playing games with you?"

"When he was ordering, it sounded like he said he wanted *my* cupcake instead of saying he wanted *a* cupcake and when I confronted him, he denied it."

"Did you really—?" Felicity shook her head.

"Yeah, I called him out on it because that's what he said."

"Maybe that's what you heard. You know you have selective hearing. Or it could've been what you *wished* he'd said since he was giving you hot flashes and all." Felicity laughed.

"It's not," Gianna responded. "Besides, he was too hot for me. He looked like one of those rich, business types—you know—the kind who come to you looking for wives because they're too busy to date."

Felicity folded her food container closed. "Gianna, why do you do that?"

"What?"

"Sell yourself short. You're beautiful, Gianna."

"Girl, please." Gianna waved her comment off. "I'm too busy hustling cupcakes to be beautiful."

"Whatever. You're beautiful and the only reason you've never been involved with anyone is because you've been working like a slave and taking care of Gemma."

"Well, somebody has to do it. She *is* my sister."

"I know, and you're right, but you have a life, too."

Gianna frowned. "What life? I've never had a life outside of Gemma. It has always been me taking care of her since mom bounced. Just me, and I refuse to abandon her just to have a *life* when she's on the verge of losing hers." Gianna blinked away the mist in her eyes and decided to change the subject. "Tell me what's going on at Wedded Bliss these days."

"Girl, I cannot stand it when these guys sign up for the program and then get cold feet. There's this one guy who came to see me a month ago. He still hasn't looked through the profiles I sent him and when I called him out on it, he said he didn't have time. And I'm racking my brain like, does this guy want a wife or not, and if he doesn't want a wife, why did he sign up for my services? It's so irritating."

"Maybe he changed his mind. That *can* happen, you know."

"Really? I charge five-hundred per application and after the application is approved, the deposit is five-thousand. Now granted, most of these men are wealthy, but fifty-five-hundred dollars is fifty-five-hundred dollars. Who has money to throw away like that?"

"Apparently some people do, and I wish they would throw some this way. Gemma's first chemotherapy treatment was seven-thousand-dollars, and that's *after* insurance."

"Oh my gosh."

"I've already taken out a second mortgage on the house, business isn't all that great at the bakery as you know, and sometimes, I don't know what I'm going to do. So it must be nice to have that much money to blow." Gianna grinned and shook her head at the unfairness of life. Some people had it like that and some people didn't, but hey, maybe they made better choices. Pursued the top paying careers that afforded them the opportunity to drive the nicest cars. Live in the nicest homes. Live without a care in the world while other people struggled to acquire life's basic necessities. "So, how many profiles did you send this guy?"

"Three. He was very particular, too particular if you ask me. He said he wanted a woman who would be loyal. She had to have a *thing* – something she enjoyed doing. And she had to have strong family ties. He said he was close with his family and couldn't have a woman disrupting his family in any way."

"Hmm…" Gianna said. "That's strange."

"Why?"

"I'm wondering why he didn't say he wanted a *beautiful* woman with hair flowing down her back. You know, what all the men say—a woman with big boobs, a big butt and a figure eight body. That's what most of them want."

"First of all, that's not what most men want."

"Okay, then let me be more specific. Most *black* men."

Felicity shook her head. "I could argue this point all day with you but I'm not going to go there. But I did find it odd that this particular guy didn't list any physical characteristics he wanted. Out of all the men I matched, all *three* of them, he was the *only* man who didn't mention anything about a woman's looks— almost like he's not really interested in the service. I don't know what to make of it. It's driving me insane."

"What are you going to do about it?"

"I told him to meet with me tomorrow if he was serious about finding a wife and he said he would, so, I guess we'll see then." Felicity stood up.

"Guess so."

"Well, I'm going to head home. I know you need your rest after the harrowing ordeal you went through today." Felicity chuckled.

"You laugh, but I need to recuperate after that."

"Yeah, because he just might show up again tomorrow. Hadn't thought about that, had you?"

"No," Gianna said and her heart immediately started beating faster.

"Maybe tall, dark and handsome really do want your cupcake." Felicity laughed as she opened the front door.

"Ugh...I hate you," Gianna said.

"Love you, too, Gianna," Felicity told her then waved before she got inside of her car.

Chapter 4

Ramsey woke up this morning with the taste of butter pecan frosting on his tongue knowing that his craving for sweets really stemmed from a desire to see the cupcake lady again. He had to know her name and anything else he could pick up on along the way.

He got up, showered and dressed in one of his finest suits. He didn't have to wear a suit today. It's not like he was going to the office. He just wanted to look extra dapper – hoping to get cupcake lady all rattled again.

He parked his black Audi A8-L in front of The Boardwalk Bakery, stepped out and buttoned his suit jacket with his left hand and proceeded inside. The bell tinkled this time, and he was surprised to see the cupcake lady – the woman he couldn't stop thinking about who was also the only woman he'd dreamed about since losing Leandra. She was standing behind the cash register. Alert. Focused.

He felt a pull to his abdomen when she looked up and connected her translucent, honey-colored gaze to his. Her eyes grew bigger. His abdomen grew tighter. In his dream, he saw her face as clearly as he was seeing it now. Yesterday, she was a nervous wreck. At a loss for words. He wondered if she was like that all the time or if she was just that way around him. He got his answer as her eyes grew even bigger as he approached the counter.

Gianna frowned slightly, then cleared her throat. She placed both hands on the counter. Cleared her throat again. Her face flushed. She tried to swallow again, but her throat was so dry, she couldn't. Felicity told her not to let a man make her flustered. That was easier said than done.

"Good morning," he said as he stood at the counter, facing her.

Oh, God. I'm going to pass out. She placed her left hand over her chest and threw up her index finger signaling that she'd be right back. She left the counter quickly and stood in the kitchen area where he couldn't see her panting.

Okay. Get yourself together, Gianna. You can't have an anxiety attack at work. He's just a man. A tall, gorgeous man towering over six feet, but still a man. It's not like he's interested in you. He's probably married. Has a girlfriend. No way he can look that good and still be single. It's impossible. Besides, he only wants cupcakes.

She took a bottle of water from the refrigerator and guzzled half of it down to relieve the dryness in her throat. She was fine before he showed up. Now, she was having hot flashes. "I'm too young to be having hot flashes," she whispered to herself.

Gathering the strength to get on with it, give him what he came for and get him out of her establishment as fast as she could, she returned to the register. He was still standing there with a smirk on his face, looking better than he looked yesterday. How was that even possible? Amazing. Today, he wore a navy blue, tailored suit with a sky blue shirt underneath and a matching necktie. His black leather shoes were so shiny, she could probably see her reflection in them.

"Let me try this again," he said. "Good morning."

She had yet to blink.

His smirked turned into a smile. "Miss?"

"Huh?" she frowned.

He chuckled. "Okay, you're really bad at this."

"At what?" she asked, seemingly spellbound staring at his mustache and lips – too timid to connect her gaze with his since he was standing so close.

"Customer service. Being friendly. Greeting your customers. I could go on."

"I'm not usually bad at this," she said. "It's just...that...um...I..." She took a breath. "I didn't expect to see you back here again today after what happened yesterday."

Curious as to what her response would be, he asked, "What happened yesterday?"

She shrugged and glanced around the empty bakery. "You know...I kinda screwed up with you...didn't make a good first impression. You thought I was psycho."

He laughed. "I didn't think you were psycho. I thought you were unduly nervous, the same way you are now."

"So, why'd you come back?"

He placed his hands on the counter and leaned towards her. "*The* cupcake has me coming back."

Gianna swallowed the lump in her throat. "Ri-right," she said. She should've known he hadn't come back to see her. Clearing her throat, she asked, "What can I get you today?"

"Do you remember what I had yesterday?"

"Yes. How could I forget? You were one of my few morning customers."

"I want the exact same thing I had yesterday, but make it a double order."

"A double order?" she asked trying not to frown, but the grimace wasn't any better. She should've known he was taken, probably by some ravishing supermodel type chick with an accent. "Is someone joining you this morning?"

The corner of his mouth lifted. "Do you think I'm going to drink two large coffees and eat two cupcakes?"

"You could. You look like a giant. You could probably eat a dozen cupcakes in one sitting."

He flashed her a playful grin. "You really speak your mind, don't you?"

She covered her mouth with her hand. "I'm sorry. I didn't realize I was saying that out loud."

He laughed. "How can you *not* realize you're talking out loud?"

"I'm, um…I'm not very good at talking."

He lifted a brow. "You're not very good at *talking*?"

"No," she answered.

"Is that why you're turning red right now?"

"Probably," she forced out.

"Do you normally have trouble conversing with men?"

"No. Just you."

"Why me?"

After a half shrug, she replied, "I don't know."

"But you don't know me."

"That's what makes this so weird. *I'm* weird. I told you that, didn't I?"

He couldn't recall if she mentioned that to him or if he'd come to the conclusion on his own. "The reason I want a double order is because, yes, someone is joining me."

"Oh, okay. Colleague? Client? Girlfriend?"

"No. You."

Gianna's eyebrows raised before she frowned. "You're kidding, right?"

"No."

"I can't join you. I have to work."

Ramsey looked around, then connected his gaze with hers. "There's nobody in here."

"Doesn't matter. I'm baking biscuits. I mean, cupcakes. I have to put frosting on the ones that are already done, fill the display case and prepare for the noon rush."

"Excuses, excuses," Ramsey said, glancing at a platinum watch on his left wrist. "It's 9:05 a.m. You have time. Come sit with me."

Gianna chewed on her bottom lip as she

considered it for a moment. She didn't know this man. Just because he bought cupcakes didn't make him a good guy. And she wasn't much for small talk with people she didn't know, especially wickedly handsome strangers.

"You're thinking too much."

She looked up at him. He was so milk chocolatey, her mouth watered for something sweet. Skip the butter pecan cupcake. She needed some chocolate in her life. Chocolate in the form of a cupcake – not the man. The cupcake. At least that's what she told herself.

She took a butter pecan cupcake from the display and set a coffee cup on the counter beside it.

"Decided not to join me, huh?" he asked.

"I may...I have to check the oven."

She rang up his purchase, and he gave her another twenty dollar bill, same as yesterday.

"I see you still don't have a tip jar," he observed.

She smiled, handing him his change. "Haven't gotten around to it. If you don't like carrying around change, you should just use a credit card. I accept those, too."

"Duly noted," he said. "But you can keep the change." He picked up his cup and the little, pink-rimmed paper plate that his cupcake was on. "I'll be over here waiting for you."

"I'm sure you will," Gianna mumbled under her breath as she went to the back, completely flustered, her stomach twisted in a million knots. Walking in circles, she said "I can't sit with him. I'm a nervous wreck. A klutz. He'll think I'm nuts. How am I going to get out of this one? Think Gianna. Think!"

When the oven buzzed, she yelled. The man had her so shook, her own oven scared the daylights out of her, so much so that she jumped clean off the floor.

"Everything okay back there?" Ramsey asked.

"Ye-yeah. Everything's fine."

"I thought I heard a scream. You didn't hurt yourself, did you?"

"No. I'm fine." Gianna took out a fresh batch of cupcakes and set the tray on a cooling rack. Then went in another batch.

Talking to herself again, she said, "Okay, Gianna. Just go out there and say a few words to him. It's no big deal. He's a customer. A dreamingly handsome customer, but still—a customer. Remember, he's not interested in you. He only wants your cupcakes."

Gianna pulled in a breath – a breath full of flour dust particles and began coughing. When she was able to get her coughs under control, she took one of the frosted, chocolate cupcakes and walked to the front. She sat down at the two-chair, round table across from the insistent gentleman.

"Where's your coffee?" he asked with a smile on his face, pleased that she joined him.

"I don't drink coffee. It makes me jittery and, as you can see, I'm already a nervous wreck all on my own. No caffeine needed."

"Why's that?"

"I just am." She dipped her index finger in

the chocolate frosting on her cupcake and brought it to her mouth, sucking it off.

Ramsey watched as she repeated this over and over again. He was certain she wasn't trying to be seductive, but that's the thing that made her actions *that* much more alluring. He couldn't look away. *Jeez. She needs to stop. Please stop. You're turning me on.* His legs bounced up and down underneath the table. *I need a distraction.* He cleared his throat and asked, "What's your name?"

"Gianna."

"Gianna," he said, smiling. He thought she had a pretty name, one he would love saying over and over again. It suited her. "What's your last name, Gianna?"

She lifted a brow. "Why?"

He chuckled. "Don't worry. I won't cyberstalk you or anything like that. Just curious."

She pulled her finger from her mouth in one long, slow lick and said, "It's Jacobsen. And you would be?"

Thoroughly intrigued. Instead of saying what he was thinking about her, he answered, "Ramsey St. Claire."

"Ramsey...sounds masculine."

"Well, I am a man, so..."

"I know. What I meant was, it sounds strong. Like the name of a man with strength. One that means business."

"Then I guess my parents could predict the future by naming me because I'm just as you describe. Strong, and I always mean business."

"Do you?" she asked licking more chocolate from her finger. She glanced up at Ramsey when he didn't respond, then looked at him again holding his gaze. "What?" she asked. She'd just swiped another glob of chocolate on the tip of her finger and was about to take it to her mouth again.

"You make it look so good, I want to try it," he said. Before she had a chance to protest, he reached for her wrist and pulled her finger towards his mouth.

She frowned. "What are you doing?"

"This," he responded right before he opened his mouth, pulling her finger between his lips and closed his warm mouth around her finger.

Her throat nearly closed up. She couldn't believe what was happening. A tingling sensation – one of which she'd never experienced before – traveled through her and pooled at her stomach. When her head had stopped spinning, she snatched her hand away from him. "Don't ever do that again! What's wrong with you? Are you some kind of sick pervert with a cupcake fetish or something?"

He wanted to laugh, but he managed to maintain a straight face when he said, "No. I'm sorry, Gianna. I just wanted to taste. That's all. Forgive me."

Her frown deepened. "You tasted my finger!"

"I apologize. Usually, women like getting this kind of attention from me."

"Well, I don't know you?" she said her cheek reddening with every passing second. "What was this? Some kind of test to see how far you could go with me?"

"No. I can assure you—"

"Assure me that you will *never* touch me again! I don't know you. Just because you're some dark chocolate god doesn't give you the right to touch me."

His eyes narrowed playfully. "Did you just call me a chocolate god?"

"Okay, I'm done," she said standing.

"Wait," he said touching her forearm before quickly snatching his hand away. "I'm sorry. I won't touch you again. My mistake."

Ramsey took a bite of his cupcake, glancing up at Gianna as she took a bite of hers. With all the chocolate frosting from her cupcake gone, she was eating the actual *cake* part of it. She was right about herself, he concluded. She *was* weird. "Tell me, Gianna—how long have you owned this place?"

"Two years."

"You must really love cupcakes."

"I love baking them more than I like eating them. I used to do this as a hobby."

"Then you decided to turn your hobby into a business."

Staring at the size of his hand, she missed his question. That hand was wrapped around her dainty wrist just a few minutes ago. Her finger was inside of his mouth. She glanced up at him and caught his eyes again. "Did you say something?"

The sound of the doorbell tinkling had her looking there. Gianna smiled warmly when she saw the visitor was Jerry.

"Excuse me for a moment," she told Ramsey, then walked over to Jerry. She embraced him. The man had on the same filthy clothes from yesterday. "Good morning, Jerry."

"Moanin', sweet thang."

"How did you like the cupcakes?"

"They were good as always. The carrot cream cheese was my favorite, though. You need to make a batch of those for rush hour today, sugar."

"I'm already on it, and I set aside some for my favorite customer. Be right back."

Gianna disappeared off into the kitchen for a moment, then she was back with a half dozen cupcakes. "Here you go. Enjoy."

"Thank you, sweetie."

"You're welcome, Jerry. Be safe out there, okay?"

"Yes, ma'am," he said while exiting.

Since there were still no other customers in the bakery, Gianna returned to her seat across from Ramsey. She glanced up at him, catching his inquisitive gaze. She quickly looked away. She still couldn't believe he'd licked her finger.

"How do you know that guy?" Ramsey inquired. Even though it was none of his business, he felt like he needed to know.

Gianna's eyes brightened. "How do I know Jerry?"

"Yes."

"Oh. Two years ago when I got motivated to get this place up and running, Jerry used to sit out front. Every day when I came by to do some painting or some other task to fix up the bakery, he was there. He looked homeless to me, and I figured he was since he would always have on the same clothes and sit in the exact same spot. So, one day, I walked over to him and sat down. I introduced myself and found out that he was indeed homeless and he was worried about having to find a new place to *stay* since he thought I would request that he relocate from the area in front of my new place of business. Instead, I gave him a red velvet cupcake."

"You gave him a cupcake?"

"I did. I had made a dozen at home the night before and something told me to take one just in case I saw him again. He's been addicted ever since. I always save some for him. The only thing is, I never know when he's going to show up."

Ramsey narrowed his eyes trying to understand her. As it was, she didn't have many customers, wasn't turning a profit (in his assumption) and she was giving away cupcakes for free?

"What?" she asked him when she saw the confused look on his face.

"Most people wouldn't do that."

"You mean most people wouldn't be nice and treat people with dignity and respect? Yeah, you're right. Most people *wouldn't* do that."

He stared at her for a moment. Gianna's heart was as good as her cupcakes. He liked that. He pulled the paper from around his cupcake to finish it. "Delicious."

"Glad you enjoyed it." Gianna took a bite of her chocolate cupcake and after chewing, she said, "Jerry's the guy who told me to start selling coffee to get more business in the mornings. It got a few people through the doors. Not much traffic, though, as you can see."

"Yeah." Ramsey took a sip of coffee. "Earlier, you said you love baking cupcakes."

"I do."

"But this," he said, looking around, "Is not your passion."

"Are you asking me or telling me?"

"Telling."

"And how do you figure that?" she asked with crumbs falling out of her mouth. "Oh, sorry. Let me go grab a napkin."

"Here's one," he said, offering it to her quickly so she couldn't get up.

"Thank you. Apparently, I don't know how to eat either."

"You're fine." *In every aspect of the word.*

"Whatever," Gianna said, knowing he was probably disgusted by her poor table manners.

Ramsey continued, "What I was saying was, I don't get the vibe that this is your passion."

"It kinda is."

"It either is, or it isn't. There's no in between when it comes to passion."

A nervous smile shaped her lips, lips that Ramsey had been watching intently. She glanced up at him curious if a man like him could really be interested in a woman like her or was he just being overly friendly? It was probably the latter. Plus, he seemed to enjoy cupcakes. Maybe he had a sweet tooth and a fetish for licking women's fingers.

His eyes narrowed. She still hadn't answered him.

Her pulse quickened by the second, but when she heard the doorbell, she jumped up from the chair, literally saved by the bell. She greeted the Caucasian brunette, a woman she'd seen in the bakery before.

"What can I get for you today?"

"Let me get a small decaf and one of your cream cheese carrot cupcakes."

"To go?"

"Yes, please.

"Okay. Coming right up." Gianna put on a serving glove and took a cupcake from the display. She put it in a cute, little pink box with her bakery's logo on it. After placing a small coffee cup on the counter, she swiped the woman's credit card and gave her a receipt.

While the woman was standing at the coffee station, Gianna went to check the oven. Then she walked back to the front counter and stood behind the register.

She watched the woman leave, then glanced over at Ramsey.

"Are you coming back, or are you scared?" he asked.

"I'm...not...scared." *Who am I kidding? I'm scared and nervous. I haven't had a conversation with a man in...O-M-G! I've never had a conversation with a man. What am I doing?* Reluctantly, she walked back over to the table and sat down.

"Now, where were we?" he asked.

"I'm not answering any more questions about my bakery until I find out a thing or two about you," she said, crossing her arms over her chest. "I mean, you come into my bakery, two days in a row now, asking questions...you could be the IRS for all I know."

He chuckled. "What if I was? You owe back taxes or something?"

"I'm not saying anything that could incriminate myself."

He grinned. "You don't have to plead the fifth with me, Gianna. I don't work for the IRS."

She gazed at him skeptically. "Then who do you work for?"

"Myself. I own an architectural firm."

Her eyebrows raised. "You're an architect?"

"I am."

"That's...that's awesome."

He smiled. "What's so awesome about it?"

"It's...um...it's something you can be proud of. Something that impresses people. People respect architects."

"People respect bakers."

"No, they don't." Gianna chuckled. "Look at me. I'm covered in flour and wear this hideous hairnet like an old lady who serves meals at a hospital cafeteria. Meanwhile, you're looking like you just walked out of GQ magazine."

"What does it matter how I look? I'm telling you...I don't know how to *make* or *bake* cupcakes and I respect the fact that you do. And you're skilled in it."

"Well, thanks, but to my point, there's nothing to making and baking cupcakes. You could learn that very easily. Designing buildings and city structures, on the other hand, is much more complicated. It takes years of schooling. Learning how to bake didn't require any schooling. It's—"

The sound of the doorbell interrupted them again. She looked at the door then glanced at Ramsey. "It's getting close to my busy time."

"I see," Ramsey said. "How about I see you at a time when you're not so busy—a time we can resume this conversation with fewer interruptions? Like, let's say dinner tonight."

Her face contorted. *Did he—? He couldn't have—? Did he just ask me out to dinner?* "Um, I'm sorry. What did you say?"

"I asked if we could resume this conversation over dinner tonight."

"Dinner?" she asked, aloof.

"Yes, dinner. You know, when people sit down in the evenings and eat a meal," he said, amused. There was something about this woman that brought out a lighter side of him. He didn't have to be so rigid the way he was at the office. The way Royal constantly complained about.

"You want to have dinner with me?" she asked to be sure he knew what he was asking.

"Yes, Gianna. I want to have dinner with you."

"Umm," her voice wavered. "I'll have to

think about it."

He reached into the pocket of his suit jacket and said, "Then take my card. Call me before five if you're interested."

"Okay," she said taking the card from his grasp, being extremely careful not to touch him. She didn't want her hand making any contact with his in any way. She stood up. "Enjoy the rest of your day."

"I will. You do the same, Gianna," he said, watching her as she walked away, looking her up and down again.

Chapter 5

RAMSEY SAT IN the front seat of his Audi and smiled. Still parked out in front of the bakery, he looked through the windows and could see Gianna working while a few more people went inside. A smile settled into the corner of his mouth. He liked her. He didn't know why she was of particular interest to him, but he liked her. Maybe it was because she was unlike any woman he'd ever encountered with her peculiar ways and rattled demeanor. While it could've been a turnoff to some men, he enjoyed it mainly because she wasn't being pretentious. She was being her, self-described, *weird* self. And she wasn't doing a thing to impress him – almost like she knew she didn't have a shot with a man like him. But the truth of the matter was, she stood a better chance than the women Felicity James wanted him to meet.

He shook his head. It frustrated him to no end to have to drive across town to talk about some women he didn't like and barely found interesting. It was obvious to him that Felicity had no clue what kind of woman he wanted. The profiles she sent were of some beautiful women, but what else did they have to offer? What made them unique? What set them apart from all the other women who gave him unwanted *obeisance* just to have a shot at a date with *the* Ramsey St. Claire? He already knew he had it like that. He didn't need praise from a woman and he definitely didn't want a woman who wanted him because he had money and looked good. He wanted a woman who wasn't influenced by his looks and wealth. Like a woman who would hug him even if he was a bum on the street instead of a well-dressed, millionaire boss. A woman like...

Dang.

He was thinking of Gianna yet again. Even when he turned into the parking structure of the building that housed Wedded Bliss – a building *he* designed – he was thinking of her. He wanted so badly to finish their conversation from earlier. Wanted to see her talk and make attempts to pretend she was at ease around him when she was anything but. He liked the way a dimple formed in her right cheek when she smiled. He loved the soothing sound of her voice. The way she chewed. He even liked the way the crumbs fell out of her mouth. Crazy, but he liked it. Things he would usually find unappealing in other women didn't bother him when it came to Gianna.

He pulled in a deep breath and snatched the manila folder from the front seat containing the profiles Felicity had emailed to him. He reckoned if he printed them out, it would serve as proof that he actually took the time to read through and study these so-called *matches*. They were anything but.

Stepping out of the car, he closed the door, hit the lock button on his keyless entry and walked up to the building as confident as he wanted to be. He spoke to a woman who was staring him down as he passed her by. He said a quick hello to another woman in the elevator who'd catch glimpses of him whenever she thought he wasn't looking.

When the elevator opened to the third floor, he got off and headed for Wedded Bliss' suite.

"Mr. St. Claire, it's good to see you again," the receptionist, a young black woman who looked like she could be an intern, greeted him as soon as he opened the door.

"Good morning. How are you?" he asked courteously.

"I'm good. Thanks for asking. Ms. James is actually ready to see you if you'll just come this way."

I'm ready to see her, too, he thought, fuming inside. Quietly, he followed her to Felicity's office and when he stepped inside, he waited for the receptionist to close the door before he walked over to Felicity's desk, slammed the folder down on it and said, "This is absolute bull!"

He didn't know his irritation would come out so soon and unfiltered but had she done her job in the first place, she'd known what kind of woman he was looking for.

Felicity frowned, taken aback. "Excuse me?" She opened the folder as he took a seat in front of her desk. She looked up at him, trying with all her might to keep her composure. She was a hair away from dropping this man as a client. She wasn't one to give up on someone, but he was making her decision so much easier. "Okay. I take it you didn't like them."

"That would be correct. Nothing about these women appealed to me. Absolutely nothing. You said my wife was in my inbox when we last spoke, so where is she? I don't see her. All I see is the profile of three women who have nothing that attracts me."

Felicity studied the hard edge of his jaw and leaned back in her seat. She'd sent him profiles of three, beautiful women with careers, so what was the problem? "Okay, Mr. St. Claire. I need you to level with me."

"About what?"

"For starters, there's a section on the intake questionnaire *you* filled out that requires you to list the features of the woman who would be perfect for you. You left it blank. Why?"

"How am I supposed to know what her features would look like?"

"Usually men have a preference. Are you telling me you don't?" she asked with raised brows.

He thought about preferences for a moment but could only see Gianna's face from this morning and that dimple he'd grown fond of. He liked her dimple. He liked her light brown eyes and how they'd change with her mood. When she was happy, they were the lightest of browns – like a ray of sunlight striking a jar of honey. Nervous, they'd darken with hints of green. And when she was angry, like when he licked her finger, they'd turn as brown as freshly brewed coffee. He smiled.

Short of snapping her fingers, Felicity said, "Mr. St. Claire?"

His smile slipped as his eyes rolled up to meet hers. "Yes?"

"Do you have a preference?" Felicity asked again.

"No."

Felicity sighed. It almost seemed like he was being difficult on purpose. "Okay. You're a thirty-nine-year-old millionaire who doesn't have a preference about the kind of woman he wants to marry. That's illogical, unreasonable and I'm not falling for it, so let me help you out. You're tall. Most tall men like short women. Do you like your woman short? Long hair? Short hair? Brown-skinned? Light? Thick, skinny or somewhere in between? You have to give me something to work with here."

Ramsey glanced at his watch.

"Mr. St. Claire?" Felicity said testily.

Ramsey stood up, slid his hands into his pockets and silently paced the area in front of her desk. "I want a woman who's easy to like. A woman who's genuine. I don't like a lot of fakeness. Fake hair, fake nails. Botox here and there. Implants. None of that. I want a real, down-to-earth, genuine woman, and Ms. James—I don't care how she looks. Looks have never been a motivating factor that would determine whether I could like someone. I see hearts, not faces. That's why I left that section blank."

She lowered her head. "Seriously?"

He stopped pacing, looked at her and said, "Yes. Seriously. In fact, I would prefer to go on your database and look for myself. Can I do that, or is that not a part of the *package*?"

Her eyes narrowed. "You certainly can do that if you have free time to search through a database that contains well over one-hundred-thousand women."

"I'm certain I can narrow the results based on search criteria."

"Yes, you can. The database *does* contain filters. Unfortunately for you, there are no filters for fake hair and all that other stuff you named, but if you would prefer to take a stab at it yourself, be my guest, Mr. St. Claire. I'll send a guest login and password to your email."

"Perfect," Ramsey said. "After I finish doing *your* job, I'll get back to you on Monday." He headed for the door.

"No, you got that all wrong, Mr. St. Claire. I did *my* job. If you don't like the results, maybe you should've fully completed your questionnaire and gotten back to me before an entire *month* passed by. You can't blame me for your inability to follow through on something *you* signed up for."

"I'll blame whoever I want to blame. Thank you for your time, Ms. James," he said quickly before exiting the office.

Felicity rolled her eyes. "What a jerk," she hissed. She was on the fence about letting him sign up when she'd first met the man. She thought something was off about him. Now she knew it for a fact. She felt sorry for the woman he'd choose to marry. He would be one of those dictator husbands. One of those, when-I-say-jump-you-say-how-high husbands. She shook her head. The sad part was, some desperate woman would take him and deal with it, all because he was rich.

Chapter 6

AT HOME, RAMSEY followed up on emails while eating pretzel chips and fresh guacamole dip made by Carson, his butler whom he liked to refer to as his personal assistant. He didn't want to indulge in a full lunch since he'd planned on eating dinner with Gianna this evening.

He glanced at the clock. The time was 1:45 p.m. and she still hadn't called him. Given her shy nature, he didn't expect her to but it would've been nice if she had pushed herself beyond her own limitations to make an effort to talk to him. At least then, he'd know she was interested. Now, he had to sit and wait until 3:30 since he'd already made up his mind that if he didn't hear from her by then, he'd be right back at the bakery. The bakery closed at 7:00 p.m. and was a forty-five-minute drive away from his house. That would give him at least two hours to spend with her.

To pass the time, he replied to a bunch of emails. He followed up with Ralph and Gilbert about the University City excavation. Ralph reassured him that the new crew would start on Monday. He set an appointment reminder on his phone to be at the site Monday morning.

The ringing of his cell phone took him out of his email-answering marathon. Could it be her? Hoping that it was, he picked up the phone and looked at the display. He sighed. It wasn't her. His brother, Regal, was the caller.

His brother!

He was supposed to pick up Regal from the airport two hours ago. Regal had been in Paris finishing out their business there – meeting with a company who wanted to hire St. Claire Architects to design a new twelve-story structure in the United States for their unique fashion line, and they wanted the business based in Charlotte. Picking Regal up from the airport would've given them time to talk face-to-face about the project, especially since they still hadn't decided whether or not to take the Paris gig.

"Regal," Ramsey answered. "I completely forgot to pick you up."

"And this is the very reason I told you we need to hire drivers. We're at that level now, Ram. It's not like we can't afford it. I had to take an Uber home."

Ramsey grinned. "You called an Uber?"

"I did. It's a good service to use, especially when your *brother*—the one who's so *anal*, he usually never forgets anything—*forgets* to pick you up from the airport."

"Why didn't you remind me, man?"

"Because I usually don't have to. What's got you so preoccupied?"

Ramsey frowned a little. He had been distracted by Gianna, but that was a good distraction. It was the nonsense with Wedded Bliss that had him off balance in addition to the delays with the University City project. "It's nothing, Regal. I'm good."

"Are you sure about that?" Regal asked.

Out of all of his brothers, he was the closest with Regal and Regal always seemed to know when something was up. "Of course. Why do you ask?"

"Some of the guys from the office said you were on a warpath."

Ramsey blew a breath. "Yeah, well they ain't seen a warpath yet. If they would do their jobs, they wouldn't have to worry about me."

"What happened this time?"

"I'll tell you about it later. Then you can catch me up to speed with the Paris deal."

"Alright. Hit me up when you get time."

"Yep," Ramsey responded. He ended the call, placing the cell phone on his desk.

With a folded hand, he held up his chin while looking at the phone, tapping his fingers on his desktop. Cupcake lady hadn't called yet, and he was growing more frustrated by the passing seconds. He couldn't roll up to the bakery with this level of frustration, so he decided to go for a run to burn off some stress. He'd normally work out in his scenic home gym, but the sunshine beckoned him outside, so he obeyed and went. Running would give him time to think about his out-of-nowhere obsession with Gianna.

While he ran, he thought about how she wasn't necessarily the type of woman who'd capture his attention. It was true what he told Felicity – he didn't have preferences per se – especially superficial ones – because he preferred to know a woman inside before ever analyzing whether or not he liked the outside which was usually a given had she passed his inner examination. But since losing Leandra, he never had a draw to examine a woman's heart or get to know her the way he wanted to know Gianna. And she had behaviors that would annoy him under normal circumstances. She was timid and jumpy—easily flustered and somewhat scatterbrained. And there were things about her that he couldn't quite understand. Like why would a woman who owned a struggling bakery just hand away cupcakes? There was no business sense in giving away goods whether you were struggling or not. And where was the company's website, Facebook page or Instagram account with mouthwatering images of her cupcakes? Cupcakes that, in his opinion, were sorely underpriced? How could she not know the value and true worth of her product? Then there was the woman herself. Who was she? He needed to know more to help him understand why she had consumed his thoughts from the moment they'd met. The connection was instant, only she hadn't felt it. But he had, and he still did.

BY THE TIME he returned home, he had just enough time to take a quick shower. Then he dressed in a pair of jeans and a burgundy polo.

"Shall I expect you home for dinner, Ramsey?" Carson asked. The fifty-five-year-old black man with a head of gray-black hair was a little shorter than Ramsey and knew how to do it all when it came to the maintenance of the house and caring for menial tasks that Ramsey didn't have the time or patience to concern himself with. And Carson cooked the most delicious meals. Now that he knew and understood Ramsey's eating habits, likes and dislikes, he would prepare whatever he chose without having to ask Ramsey what he wanted.

"No, Carson. I'll eat dinner before I return."

"Are there any pertinent matters you need handled before your return?"

"Yes. This isn't pressing but can you arrange to have all the windows cleaned inside and out? I know it was just done a week ago, but they don't look clean enough for me. Try a new cleaning agency this time. Any day of the week is fine with me." Ramsey was a stickler for a clean house. For overall organization period.

"Yes. I'll get right on it. Enjoy your evening, Ramsey."

"You do the same, Carson."

On the way to the car, Ramsey checked his phone again. Still, no calls from Gianna. He didn't get it. Normally, women jumped at the chance to call him. Women jumped at the chance to do *anything* concerning him, but Gianna hadn't bothered. Now, she wouldn't have to.

* * *

He pulled up at the bakery and through the front window, he could see that the place was barren. Bad for her. Good for him. It would give them more time to finish where they'd left off this morning.

When he walked in, the annoying doorbell tinkled but she was nowhere in sight.

"Hello? Anybody home?" he called out.

"Just a sec," she yelled from the back.

He couldn't see her, but he heard her. And then she came strolling to the front still wearing the black, flour-dusted apron from this morning, carrying a large box of cupcakes.

When Gianna looked up and saw that it was Ramsey, her breath caught in her throat and she lost all control of her own body. Her hands joggled, and the box slipped right through her fingers, crashing to the floor.

"Crap!" she yelled. She stooped down to clean up the mess. Lemon cupcakes spilled out everywhere.

"Here. Let me help you with that," Ramsey said, coming to her aid by inviting himself behind the counter.

"No, I got it," she said irritably. Frowning, she asked, "What are you doing here, anyway?"

"What are you doing carrying two dozen cupcakes?"

"It's my job. It's not like they're heavy."

"Then why'd you drop the box?"

Because you make me nervous. That's why.
"Because you startled me."

"How did I startle you when I announced my arrival?"

"I thought you were the customer coming to pick them up. That's why I was bringing the box to the front," she said, tossing more ruined cupcakes into the box that she now had to throw away. "Now, I have to rush to frost another twenty-four cupcakes before my customer arrives, which is any minute now. I hate rushing...I can't stand feeling anxious. Every single day of my life I'm a mess and now you come bothering me all the time. I need to work. I need to focus. I can't focus with you around," she said tossing the last cupcake inside of the box.

Ignoring her, he said, "I'll help you frost more cupcakes, okay. Just show me what to do."

Gianna sighed heavily with reddened, clammy cheeks. "I got it." She took the box of mangled cupcakes to the trash, then washed her hands and began frosting the extras she'd baked. Thank goodness she had. Otherwise, she would have a disappointed customer and with business already slow, she couldn't afford to lose any of her catering customers.

Walking up behind her, Ramsey said, "Tell me what I can do to help."

"Oh, goodness," she said, her pulse quickening since she was unaware that he was standing so close to her. "Okay. If you want to help, can you clean up that mess?" Gianna asked, pointing to the yellow icing on the ceramic tiled floor.

"Sure," he said. "I'm really sorry about this."

Ramsey found his way around the kitchen, grabbed paper towels and cleaned up the frosting from the floor.

"It doesn't have to be perfect," Gianna told him. "I mop the floors before I leave."

"Okay," he said, but continued cleaning up the area until it was no longer slippery. He threw the dirty paper towels in the garbage and washed his hands. Then he stood a few feet away from Gianna, watching as she rushed to add lemon frosting to more cupcakes while holding something that looked like a bag with a metal tip on it, squeezing the frosting out. He could see that her hands were still unsteady, but she was forcing them as steady as she could hold them in order to finish adding the frosting.

"Why did you drop the box, Gianna?" he asked.

"I told you...you scared me. I didn't expect to see you here, at least not during this time of the day. And you have on *normal* clothes."

His forehead creased. "And that scared you?"

Ugh. Leave me alone and stop asking so many questions so I can concentrate. "I told you I'm a train wreck. Why are you here, anyway?"

"I knew you wouldn't call me. That's why I'm here."

She glanced over at him, her darkened eyes filled with irritation. Had he stayed home or wherever he was before deciding to show up here, she wouldn't have to work twice as hard for the same amount of pay. "Well, I have to finish up this order and customers are not allowed in the kitchen."

Ramsey threw his palms up. "Okay. Fine." He strolled back to the front and sat at his usual table when a woman came inside.

Gianna hoped the bell was the sound of Ramsey leaving. When she peeped and saw a customer standing at the register and Ramsey sitting at a table, she sighed. She walked to the checkout counter.

"Hey, there," Gianna said, greeting her customer.

"Hi. I came for the six-dozen, lemon cupcakes."

"Okay. I'm actually frosting the last dozen."

"Oh. I thought they would've been ready by now."

"Almost. Just five more minutes, okay. I'm really sorry about the delay."

"Okay. Not a problem."

Gianna returned to the kitchen to resume frosting the last few then carefully began placing them all in a new box, two at a time. She brought two boxes to the front counter, followed by the third one she had to remake thanks to Ramsey.

"Okay," she said sounding breathless. After plugging the figures in the cash register, she said, "With tax, your total comes to $199.53."

Holding her wallet in her left hand, the woman slid out a credit card and handed it to Gianna.

After swiping it, Gianna handed it back to her, then gave her a pen so she could sign the receipt. "Thank you, and again, I apologize for the delay."

"No problem, dear," the woman said, placing her wallet back inside of her purse.

"Can I help you take these out to your car?"

"If you don't mind," the woman responded.

"No. Not at all." Gianna picked up one of the boxes again.

Ramsey tried not to stare, he really tried, but he couldn't help himself. She already looked nervous and her hands were shaking again. To ease her nerves, he stood up and walked to the door, holding it open for the women. Then he followed them outside and down the sidewalk to the woman's car.

"You got it?" he asked Gianna, walking directly behind her.

"Yes. I got it this time," she replied.

The customer unlocked the doors to a silver, Toyota, RAV4.

"I'll get the door for you," Ramsey said. "Front or back?"

"I'm just going to sit them on the back seat," the customer responded.

Ramsey opened the back door and the woman lowered two boxes on the back seat. She looked at Gianna and asked, "It is okay if I stack them, correct?"

"Yes. The boxes are sturdy. They won't give."

"Perfect," she said as Gianna handed her the third box. "Thank you so much. The kids are going to love these."

"You're welcome," Gianna said. "Have a good evening."

"You do the same."

With that, Gianna walked back toward the bakery with Ramsey falling in stride beside her.

"I can't get a thank-you-for-helping-me, Ramsey?" he asked her.

He was the one who caused her this extra work and stress. Now, he wanted a thank you? Seriously? She rolled her eyes. "Thank you for helping me, Ramsey," she said, reaching for the door handle until he clutched her dainty wrist and lowered her arm.

"What are you doing?" she asked.

He snatched his hand away from her. "Sorry for touching you. I just wanted to open the door. When a lady is accompanied by a man, she's not supposed to open her own door." He pulled the door handle then said, "After you."

"Thanks." She stepped inside and glanced at the clock: 4:50 p.m. She had roughly two hours before closing. She walked behind the counter and put her customer's signed receipt in the correct compartment of the cash register.

"Am I still not allowed back there?" Ramsey asked.

"No, you're not," she said, trying to keep an even tone and expressionless face so Ramsey wouldn't know he was actually getting to her.

He leaned against the checkout counter. "Your hands are not steady," he said.

"I'm tired. I've been on my feet most of the day."

"Have you had anything to eat?"

"Uh…I don't typically eat breakfast and I was so busy at lunch, I just skipped it."

"Well, you need to eat and since you won't go out to dinner with me, I'll bring dinner to you."

"Please don't do that."

"Why not?"

"Because I—I have closing work to do here and I don't have time to have dinner." *With you.*

Ramsey checked his watch. "You close at seven, right?"

"Yes."

"It's only five o'clock and don't worry about your closing work. I'll help you out."

"I don't need your help, Ramsey."

"I'm going to help you, anyway."

Exasperated, Gianna asked, "Will you stop?" She looked up from the register and connected her gaze to his. "Why are you harassing me?"

He frowned and darted his head back. Was she serious? "I'm not *harassing* you. I'm offering my help to you."

"Well, I don't need your help. I didn't ask for your help. This is *my* bakery. Mine. And I *do not* want to have dinner with you. I don't know how much clearer I can be."

He stared at her for a long moment, then silently turned and walked away.

Finally, Gianna thought, trying to steady her beating heart while breathing a sigh of relief. After a long, stressful day, she didn't want to feel her nerves being wrecked because of his unwanted attention. It was bad enough she didn't know how to behave around him. Around any man for that matter. She'd never had to concern herself with this kind of attention before and she didn't want to do it now.

Returning to the kitchen, she packed up the leftover cupcakes to drop them off at the homeless shelter. The ones in the display case would remain there until closing just in case she had any more customers. If not, she'd pack them up as well. She never carried cupcakes over to the next day. Each day, she made a fresh batch.

As she finished packing up the final box, two dozen total of all different flavors, she heard the doorbell again. She walked to the front to greet the customer when she saw that it was Ramsey again. He placed a white, plastic bag with two takeout containers on the table – his favorite table. Her stomach bottomed out when he looked at her with dark, deep black eyes and smiled.

"Do you not understand the meaning of the word, 'no'?"

"I understand that you haven't eaten, which means your blood sugar is lower than what it should be. That's why your hands are unsteady. Why you're moody."

"I'm not moody."

"You are. You said you've been on your feet all day. I'm giving you the opportunity to sit down and have a meal with me."

Gianna pondered his reasoning. He took it upon himself to bring her some dinner and she didn't want to be rude. Still, she was annoyed. "Fine." Reluctantly, she walked over to the table and sat down.

Ramsey took a takeout tray from the bag and set it in front of her.

"It smells good. What is it?"

"It's Vietnamese food – noodles, pork spring rolls, and grilled shrimp. I got it from that Vietnamese restaurant right across the boardwalk bridge."

"The bridge by the Hilton Hotel?"

"No. The bridge by the paddle boat rental. It's called Saigon Bay. Have you ever eaten there?"

"No. I'm not all that adventurous when it comes to food or anything else. I stick to what I know and leave it at that."

"Well, that's no fun."

When she heard her phone buzz, she took it from a pocket on her apron and saw the text from her sister.

Gemma: No need to rush home. Felicity brought me some soup.

Gianna smiled, relieved. Still, she couldn't wait to get home and check on her sister. She glanced up at Ramsey. "Excuse me a moment."

"Take your time," he said then leaned back in the chair watching her as she texted. He wouldn't touch his food until she put her phone away. He wanted her full attention.

Gianna: Good. Are you feeling okay?"

Gemma: Yes, for the 10th time today, Gianna. I think this is a new record. Stop worrying so much.
Gianna: It's my job to worry!! I love u 2 pieces.

After inserting an emoji face blowing a kiss, she sent the message and placed her phone back inside the pocket on her apron and looked up at Ramsey. He was staring at her intently, so much so that she shied away.

"Everything alright?" he asked. He couldn't help but wonder who she was texting.

"Yep." She opened the tray and tasted the food. "Mmm...good," she said after trying the shrimp, eating faster to ease hunger pangs.

Ramsey purposely didn't say a word. He wanted her to eat to her satisfaction before conversation ensued.

"Did I thank you for bringing this?" she mumbled with a mouth full.

"No," he answered, biting into a pork spring roll afterward.

"Well, thank you."

"You're welcome, Gianna," he told her. This early dinner was going to be an awkward one if he couldn't get her to open up to him, or at the very least have a conversation that involved more than a few words here and a few there.

"And, FYI, your whole low blood sugar theory is not why I dropped that box," she said.

His eyebrows raised. "It's not?"

"No."

"Then why'd you drop it?"

"I told you why. It's because you make me nervous."

"Explain," he said. His dark eyes narrowed in anticipation of her response. He knew very well what his presence did to women. It happened too often for him not to recognize it.

"I don't know how to explain it exactly. It's just your presence. Your intense dark eyes. Your lips. Your smell. Your everything. You make me nervous. Being around you makes me uneasy. You're very intimidating, Ramsey, at least to a woman like me, but somehow I'm sure I'm not the first woman to tell you this."

"Actually you are," he said wiping his mouth with a white napkin.

"No way."

"Way. Other women may *think* it, but they've never come out and just said it, like you."

"Oh. Maybe I should've just kept my mouth closed, then."

"No. Your honesty is refreshing. What else don't you like about me?"

She giggled. "I didn't say I didn't like it."

"You certainly didn't say that you did."

"I know...I guess what I'm saying is, it's a lot easier for me *not* to be around you. I'm not used to this much attention from a man."

"Now that I don't believe. You mean to tell me men don't try to get your attention?"

She smiled. "I'm flattered, Ramsey. Really. But take a good look at me. Have you ever heard the expression 'hot mess'?"

He grinned. "I have."

"Well, that's me. I'm a mess. This is what I look like six days a week."

Staring at her, he couldn't see her point. There was something there...something that he could almost feel deep within her that made her the sweet, beautiful woman he wanted to know.

"Ramsey?"

He blinked. "Sorry. I was lost in thought. But, as I was saying...you can't convince me that men don't try to come on to you."

"They do. Men come in here all the time—handsome men, businessmen, blue collar workers—but none of them has ever made me as anxious and nervous as you make me."

A curious glow shone in his eyes. "Why do you think that is?"

Gianna shrugged. "I'm not sure." She glanced up at him, catching the straight line of his nose and his perfectly shaped mustache before looking back down at her plate.

"So, that's why you won't go out to dinner with me?"

"Yes. Part of it."

"What's the other part?" he probed, closing his takeout container.

"I have obligations."

"The bakery?"

"Yes, and more."

"Like what?" he asked and didn't care if she heard the desperation in his voice. "Do you have children?"

Gianna snorted then covered her mouth with her hand while she laughed.

Ramsey's gaze narrowed. "No?"

"Definitely not," she said, amused. "You have to have sex to have children and I've never—" Her voice faded, and she stopped speaking when she realized she'd said too much.

Ramsey frowned not believing what she said, or was about to say, but why would she have a reason to lie about it? "So, no children?"

"No. No children," she said, although Gemma felt like a child at times. She'd been taking care of her for as long as she could remember.

"Then what other obligations do you have? Your sister?"

Gianna grimaced. Was he reading her thoughts or what? He was staring hard enough to be able to.

Ramsey knew he'd hit a nerve. Something was up with her sister. He wanted to know what it was. "Gianna?"

"Um...it's personal." Diverting, she said, "I don't understand why you want to have dinner with me. And I don't get why you're here like you have nothing better to do with your time."

"I own my own business. I decide how I spend my time. Right now, I'm spending it with you."

"Why?" she asked then nervously chewed on her bottom lip.

His eyes settled there and he couldn't help but wonder if those lips had ever been kissed. If they felt as soft as they looked. Forcing his gaze away from her lips to her eyes, he responded,

"Because I find you interesting, Gianna."

Gianna shook her head. "I'm not all that interesting. I bake cupcakes. Nothing about that is proprietary and definitely isn't appealing enough to interest an architect who owns and operates a million-dollar company."

Ramsey's narrowed gaze turned into a glare. He just wasn't accustomed to being talked to this way, but she could get away with it. And he *did* owe her an explanation so he said, "Okay. I'm here because there's something about you—some *force* pulling me to you for some reason."

Gianna lifted a brow. "Say what?"

Explaining further, he said, "From the moment I met you yesterday, I haven't been able to stop thinking about you. I wasn't supposed to walk into this bakery, but on my way to a property, I drove here, parked out front and walked right into your bakery. Now, usually I would just run through the drive-thru at the Starbucks down the street for coffee, but I came here, parked and got out."

"You must've come to the boardwalk for a specific reason."

"No, I didn't. That's what I'm trying to explain to you. When I stepped out of my car, I saw the coffee sign on your window, so I came inside and a feeling came over me. I saw you on the phone and when you turned around, when my eyes connected with yours, that feeling intensified."

"That doesn't make any sense."

"It makes perfect sense. You don't believe

the universe has a way of making sure certain people connect?"

"Yes. It's called Facebook." She grinned.

Smiling, he said, "You know what I mean."

"I do know what you mean, but uh—" Gianna stammered, not knowing how to answer his question. If the universe *did* have a way of making sure people connected why was it *him* being connected with *her*?

"Well, I do. I'm here for a reason. I want to find out what that reason is, Gianna."

"I—I don't know what to tell you."

"You think I'm crazy, don't you?"

"A lil' bit," she admitted, cracking a small smile. "Um, wow. Okay." She stood up. "I have to get this place cleaned up so—"

"I'll help you," he said standing, gathering their food trays and napkins. "What do you need me to do?"

She smiled. "Ramsey, I can handle this. I do this every day."

"What do you need me to do?"

"Okay, since you insist…can you flip the sign on the front door to *Closed* and lock the door for me?"

"Sure."

While he handled that task, she took their trash and disposed of it in the garbage can in the back.

She checked the ovens, making sure they were turned off. She wiped down the counters and took the dishes from the dishwasher. Holding a pot in her hand, she turned around to see Ramsey standing immediately behind her. The pot slipped from her grasp and he caught it before it hit the floor.

"How long were you standing there?" she asked, her heart beating out of control.

"For a few minutes."

"Why didn't you say anything?"

"Because I like watching you work. Where does this pot go?"

Gianna pointed to the hook on the wall.

Ramsey hung it there, then looked at her. "I don't like you being so nervous around me."

"I don't know you that well."

"And you won't get to know me if you refuse to talk to me," he told her.

"We just had an hour-long conversation."

"Yes, but I need more time with you."

"More? I don't have time for anything more."

"What do you want me to do, sweet thang? Beg?"

She grinned knowing he got the 'sweet thang' nickname from Jerry. "You look like the kind of man who doesn't have to *beg* for anything."

"You're right, but I'll make an exception for you."

Gianna shook her head.

"Have dinner with me tomorrow night, Gianna, and I won't take no for an answer."

She chewed on her lip again.

"Say yes," he whispered, his sable eyes fixated on her mouth.

"Okay," she said. "Yes."

"You're not just saying that to get rid of me,

are you?"

She smiled. "No. We can have dinner tomorrow."

"Good." He took out his wallet and removed two one-hundred dollar bills, placing it in her hand. "This should cover the box of cupcakes you dropped."

"Oh, that's not necessary, Ramsey," she said, handing it back to him.

"It is. You're running a business, and since it was *my* fault you dropped the box, I owe you."

"But—"

"I'm not taking it back," he cut her off to say.

"Okay," she said, sliding the bills in the front right pocket of her pants. "Thank you."

"You're welcome. Is there anything else you need to do before leaving?"

"Yes. I need to sweep and mop the floors."

"How about I sweep and you mop?"

Gianna smiled. "You're going to sweep?"

"Yes. I know how to sweep."

"I don't doubt that. You just look like the kind of man who doesn't sweep."

"I don't, usually, but I'll make an exception for you. Now, do we have a deal?"

"Deal."

Ramsey took the broom and dust pan to the front and when he was done, Gianna mopped the area.

After sweeping the kitchen, Ramsey took it upon himself to take out the garbage while Gianna finished mopping.

"Is that all, boss?" he asked jokingly.

"Yes. That's all. You can exit out the back

with me and walk around the corner to your car."

"That's fine. In fact, I'd prefer to walk you to your car." He headed for the door and opened it, allowing her to exit first.

Once he was outside, Gianna locked the rear door and made sure it was secure.

"Where are you off to now?" he asked, sliding his thumb inside the pockets of his jeans.

"I'm going home. What about you?"

"I'll probably swing by my brother's place."

Her eyes lit up. "You have a brother?"

"I have three brothers, actually."

"Older or younger?"

He smiled. "See, this is why we need to see each other again. You want to know more about me, too. I don't know why you were trying to front like you won't feelin' me."

She felt blood rush to her cheeks. "I just asked a simple question."

"They're all younger than me," he said, answering her question. "What about your sister? Older or younger?"

"She's younger."

"What's her name?"

"Gemma."

"Gianna and Gemma," he said. "Sounds like a pair of troublemakers."

She smiled. "We're everything but—" she responded, looking down at her shoes feeling somewhat embarrassed by the ability he had to make her blush so hard. "What about your brothers? What are their names?"

"I'll tell you when we're at dinner."

Her mouth fell open. "No fair."

"It *is* fair. It was like pulling teeth to get you to say yes to dinner. Now, we have something to talk about when we get there, you know, so it's not awkward for you."

"I guess," she said.

"I need your number," he said, handing her his phone. "Key it in for me, please."

She did and pressed send afterward. Then her phone rang. "There you go."

When she handed him his phone back, Ramsey saved her number under 'Cupcake' in his contacts, smiling after he did so. "I probably won't get a chance to come by here tomorrow. I have a thing with the folks, so—"

"Oh. No need to explain."

"It probably comes as a relief to you anyway, huh?"

She grinned. "Yes. It does."

He laughed at her honesty.

"Anyway, I have to get going now. Thanks for your help today, Ramsey."

"Anytime, Gianna."

They stood facing each other awkwardly for a few seconds until Gianna turned away to unlock her car door.

Ramsey reached around her to grasp the handle, opening it for her. "I'll call you later," he said.

"Okay," she replied as she sat down.

"When I do, I want you to answer."

She smiled harder. "I will."

"Promise me."

"What?" she asked, looking up at him.

"You seem like a woman of your word. Promise me."

"O-kay. I promise. I will answer the phone when you call."

"Alright. Drive safe." Ramsey finally closed the door, then watched her start the SUV and drive away.

Chapter 7

RAMSEY PULLED UP at Regal's house. He got out of his car, jogged up the front steps and pressed the doorbell expecting Regal's housekeeper, Primrose – a black woman in her late fifties – to answer the door. Primrose wasn't a live-in housekeeper like Carson was a live-in personal assistant. Regal hired her for the chore side of maintaining his home than anything else. She didn't cook and rarely ran errands. Her job was to make sure the house was clean and tidy.

When the door slowly opened, it revealed the heavyset woman standing there with a dust cloth in her hand.

"Hi, Primrose."

"Hey there, Ramsey."

"Is my big head brother here?"

Primrose grinned. "Yes. Come on in. He's in the dining room eating dinner."

"Don't tell me Regal tried his hand in the kitchen," Ramsey quipped.

"Honey, if you catch Regal in the kitchen, let me know so I can document it," Primrose said.

Ramsey chuckled.

"I actually picked up some chicken with all the fixings earlier," Primrose went on to say. "I just warmed him up a plate full. He came back from Paris extra hungry. I can whip you up a plate if you would like."

"No, thanks. I've already had dinner." Ramsey continued on inside to the dining room, watching as Regal sat alone at the eighteen-chair, massive dining room table all alone. "Hey. What's up, Ram?"

Regal fist bumped with his brother. "I thought that was you ringing my doorbell at dinner time. What's going on with you?"

"Nothing much."

"Uh huh...nothing much, but your face says otherwise."

"My face ain't saying nothing." Ramsey pulled out a chair directly across from where Regal sat. He flopped down and sighed.

"I take it you're here to talk about the Paris deal, then," Regal mumbled after biting into a biscuit.

"Not exactly."

Regal fixed his narrowed gaze on his brother. "No?"

"No."

"Then what's up, Ram? The team told me you took some time off. It was news to me."

"Regal, before I left Paris I told you I was taking time off. You don't remember?"

"I do, but you're always crying wolf about taking time off. It usually never happens."

"Well, this time it did. I took a month. I'll be answering some emails from home, but I have to be on site at the University City project first thing Monday morning. I still can't believe excavation hasn't been completed there."

"Royal told me you chewed him out about it."

"He didn't leave me much choice. When something goes wrong at a site, I need to know about it. No exceptions."

Regal wiped his mouth then took a swig of sweet tea before he said, "Yeah, Ram, but to Royal's point, we do have a little time to play with when it comes to U-City."

"Time is money. We should never look at a project like we're ahead of schedule."

Regal nodded. "Because something could go wrong further up the road that we can't avoid."

"Exactly. Now, try explaining that to Royal. I swear sometimes he acts like *he* started this company."

Regal chuckled. "That's Royal. You're not *really* going to fire him are you?"

"Nah, I'm not going to fire him. I think about it constantly, but I'm not going to do it. He just needs to get with the program. That's all."

"You've always been hard on him."

"That's because I need to be. He thinks everything comes so easily since this job was pretty much waiting for him right out of college. It took a lot of hard work to get St. Claire Architects to where it is today."

"Yeah, I know. I was right there with you." Regal took a gulp of tea. "So tell me what has you so occupied that you forget to pick up your brother from the airport?"

Ramsey smirked and leaned back in his chair. "You wouldn't believe me if I told you."

"I would. I believed you when you told me you signed up for that Wedded Bliss nonsense."

"No, you didn't."

"I did. I'll admit, it was hard to believe, at first, but you convinced me. Have you found your *perfect* spouse? Is that the reason you couldn't come up for air?"

"No. I mean, yes," Ramsey said. "Well, maybe."

"Maybe?" Regal sat up tall. "I know how particular you are, so do you mean she's perfect on the inside?"

"I believe so. That's what I intend to find out." Ramsey smiled as he often did thinking about Gianna and how they'd shared dinner together at her bakery and talked. For some reason, he felt like he could talk to her for hours at a time with her body nestled close to his while he stroked her hair and stared into her gorgeous eyes.

"Ram?" Regal said to get his brother's attention.

Ramsey blinked, then looked at Regal. "Yeah?"

"I asked you why you're smiling."

"I was thinking about her."

Regal tilted his head, having a hard time understanding his brother's sudden infatuation. "Her, who? What's her name?"

"Gianna."

"And tell me what's so special about Gianna that has my normally mean, ill-tempered, inflexible brother smiling."

Ramsey didn't refute Regal's description of

him. He heard what he said, but he was too busy thinking about the way Gianna smiled and her shyness that he adored. It was a major turn-on for him when usually, timid women were a turn off. And he couldn't wait to take her out to dinner – to see her in something other than her work uniform.

Ramsey looked at his brother. "I'm smiling because I haven't felt this way about a woman since Leandra."

"Whoa." Regal wiped his mouth and pushed the rest of his food away. He knew how much Ramsey loved Leandra. She was the only woman his brother had ever loved. "I don't think I heard you right."

"You did," Ramsey said his expression serious.

"But you said you couldn't feel a connection with a woman after Leandra. It's been what? Fifteen years since she passed?"

"Yes. Fifteen years."

Regal frowned. "Are you feeling okay, Ram?"

"I'm fine," Ramsey said with a chuckle.

"I'm only asking because, in fifteen years, you've been through some gorgeous, successful, hot women—none of which you've tried to get serious with, but all of a sudden you sign up for this matchmaking service and magically find the perfect woman."

"That's just the thing. I didn't find her from Wedded Bliss. We met organically."

"How so?"

"She owns a bakery, and yesterday morning I stopped by."

"You're full of crap, man."

"I'm serious. I stopped by her bakery. That's how we met."

"But you hate sweets."

"Correction...I *used to* hate sweets. You should taste her butter pecan cupcakes. They're addictive." *Like her*.

Regal scrunched up his face. "And you met her yesterday morning? You're comparing a woman you met *two* days ago to Leandra?"

"I'm not comparing the two. I sense something with Gianna that I haven't felt in a long time. Something brought us together."

"Something like what?"

"I don't know yet, but I intend to find out."

Regal looked at his brother skeptically. He couldn't count the women Ramsey had dated in the fifteen years since Leandra had died. He found it hard to believe that not a single one stood a chance of stealing Ramsey's heart. But after witnessing it for himself, not one of them ever did. Ramsey had once told him that his heart was broken permanently since it was made to love only one woman. When that woman died, so did his desire to love again.

"I know you have this weird standard for the women you date but are you attracted to Gianna physically?"

"I'm more attracted to her soul," Ramsey responded.

"But that doesn't answer my question," Regal said. "And just how does a person become attracted to someone's soul?"

"Come on, Regal. You know how it is to meet

someone, a stranger, and you feel some strange force pulling you to that person, even though you don't actually know them."

Regal laughed. "No, I don't know how that is."

"Okay, say for instance, you're on a jog and make eye contact with a woman, nod to her when you pass and later a feeling comes over you like you have some sort of affinity with her. Like you two are in sync even though you don't know each other."

"That's called attraction," Regal said.

"No, it's not. Attraction in today's world is all physical. I'm talking something deeper than physicalities."

"Okay. Then you're attracted to her personality is what you're saying. Her energy."

"If you want to put it that way, then, yes."

"And how does Gianna feel about you?"

Ramsey chuckled. "I have no doubt in my mind that she thinks I'm irrational and crazy."

"Then, I'm with her. I like Gianna already." Regal laughed. "Seriously, though, Ramsey—I thought the whole point of you signing up at Wedded Bliss was to find an *insta*wife, a companion. Someone you could respect and treat with dignity but never love since you told me you were incapable of falling in love again. Now, all of a sudden, you're besotted by this Gianna person."

"What can I say? I couldn't help myself. My *attraction* to her soul was instantaneous."

"So, am I correct to assume that the Wedded Bliss thing is no more?"

"I'm terminating the agreement on Monday since I already have an appointment with them on the calendar for that day. It wasn't working out, anyway. Get this – the owner sent me three matches for women who, no lie, looked plastic."

Regal chuckled.

"If I wanted a blow-up doll, I'll go out and buy one."

"Ay, maybe that's what you need...something that can't love you back."

Ramsey grinned. "Whatever, man. I just can't deal with fakeness and I definitely don't want a woman who's so obsessed with the way she looks that she'd go so far as to have surgery and facelifts. I'm not into all that. I tried to explain that to the owner of Wedded Bliss and she looked at me like I was speaking German. So, I told her I'd go on their website and find my own match."

"Let me guess...you never got around to looking for a match because of Gianna."

A grin formed on Ramsey's face then widened.

"But hold on...pump the brakes," Regal said. "Did you check Wedded Bliss to see if Gianna was on there?"

Ramsey frowned. "No, but I'm positive she's not. She doesn't date."

"That's what she told you, huh?"

"Yes, and before you ask, I believe her."

Regal nodded since his brother seemed so confident about it, but he couldn't, for the life of him, get past the fact that Ramsey had just met her yesterday. "When will you see her again?"

"Tomorrow. I've finally convinced her to go out with me."

Regal's eyebrows raised. "You had to *convince* a woman to have dinner with you?"

"Odd, right?"

"Indeed, considering how women usually throw panties at you when they see you coming."

Ramsey chuckled. "You're getting me confused with yourself. Ain't no telling what you've been doing in Paris."

"Ay, what happens in Paris, stays in Paris."

"If you say so."

Ramsey stood up and said, "I have to get going. Gianna's expecting a phone call from me and I don't want to call her too late."

"Alright, man. I hope you know what you're doing." Regal stood up and walked with his brother toward the door. "And we still need to talk about Paris."

"What's your gut feeling about the project?" Ramsey asked.

Regal sighed. "Well, with all the intricacies they want in the building's design, it'll probably be the longest project we've ever taken on."

"It sounds like you're leaning towards not taking it."

Regal opened the front door, and they both stepped outside. Then he said, "My concern is that while we're spending two years on one project that will yield a ten-million-dollar profit, we could've taken on several projects that could nearly triple that."

Ramsey nodded. "That's a good point...definitely something to think about."

"Yeah," Regal said, sliding his hands into the pockets of his slacks. He looked out into the driveway at Ramsey's car. "How are you liking the new Audi?"

"It's a hot ride. Leather seats with ventilation and massage systems, the panoramic sunroof, GPS, the sound system, LED cabin lighting...what's there not to like?"

"You'll have to let me take it for a spin so I can make up my mind whether I want to get one."

"Yeah, man. Stop by the crib later on this week."

"Alright. I will."

Ramsey slapped hands with his brother. "Be easy," he told him, then began walking down the steps leading to the ground.

"Ay, I'll try to be out there at the site on Monday to make sure you don't tear someone's head off."

Ramsey chuckled. "Everybody knows you don't get up before nine o'clock."

"True, but I need to make an exception for this."

Ramsey pressed the keyless entry button to unlock his car doors. "Sure you will." He opened the car door and said, "Later."

Regal threw up a hand in a single wave, then turned around and walked back inside.

Chapter 8

"GIANNA, DO YOU remember when we were younger?" Gemma asked, with sleep-filled eyes as she rested her head on Gianna's thighs. They were on the living room sofa, had just finished watching their favorite show and Gianna had powered off the TV.

"How young are you talking?" she asked, twirling the loose end of Gianna's headscarf with her index finger. "Keep in mind I'm nine and a half years older than you, Gem."

"I know. I know. I'm talking about when I was nine and you were like nineteen."

"Okay. What about it?"

"Mom was always in and out of the house. Every time I looked up, there was a different man."

"Yeah. That was mom, alright." Gianna shook her head.

"I remember how paranoid you were to go to college because you were afraid to leave me home with her."

"More like afraid to leave you home alone."

"Yeah," Gemma grinned. "Home alone. And you didn't go to college. You stayed, because of me."

Gianna smiled remembering.

"Do you regret it?" Gemma asked.

"No, Gem. Why would I regret it? I did the right thing. Even to this day, mom is nowhere to be found. We don't even know if she's still alive. So, yes, I did the right thing."

Gemma smiled lazily. "You could have," she said faintly then started over again. "You could have been so much without me around."

"Gemma, don't say that."

"It's true," Gemma said, sitting up, facing her sister now. "Your life is wasting away along with mine, and I wish you didn't have to go through this." A tear rolled down her cheek.

"I don't mind taking care of you. You're my sister, and I love you." Gianna fought back tears. "And you're the one who shouldn't have to go through this...this stupid cancer. There's no reason, whatsoever for you to feel sorry for me." Gianna left a kiss on her sister's cheek then looked at her and smiled. "Come on. Let's get you to bed."

Gianna followed Gemma to her bedroom and said, "Goodnight, sis."

"Goodnight," Gemma replied.

Gianna closed the door, taking a deep breath leaning up against the door as tears welled up in her eyes. Then she continued upstairs to her bedroom. She felt a sense of helplessness when it came to taking care of Gemma. Most days she had to summon the strength to do so. After working all day at the bakery, she still had to clock in when she arrived home to be her sister's primary caregiver. Every day she convinced herself that she could do it – that

God would help give her the strength to keep going. But tonight – tonight was difficult. Tonight, she felt too weak to continue. It was one of those nights at the end of a stressful day where she felt she had more on her plate than she could bear alone. Tonight was overwhelming. Tonight, she couldn't hold back the tears.

She wiped them away, pulling in a breath afterward to force her body to absorb her sadness. As usual, it worked. She was used to the routine. *Okay. Breathe, Gianna. You can't afford to fall apart. Gemma needs you.*

She sat on the bed, close to the nightstand and screwed the cap off of her multivitamins, throwing a pill inside of her mouth. Just as she was about to take a sleeping pill, her phone rang. She looked at the display on her cell and saw that the caller was RSC. That's what she saved Ramsey St. Claire's name under in her phone. What was he doing calling her tonight? She didn't expect him to call tonight.

She chewed on her lip. To answer the phone or not answer the phone. That was the question. But why was she even considering *not* answering when she promised him she would? So, clearing her throat and plastering a smile on her face in hopes to put herself in a better mood, she answered, "Hello?"

"Hey, cupcake."

Gianna's fake smile was instantly replaced by a genuine one. "Hey. I didn't expect you to call me tonight."

"I didn't tell you when I would call."

"So, you chose to call me 10:32 at night?"

"Yes. You're not in bed this early, are you?"

"Almost." She sniffled. "I was taking my vitamins."

"Are you okay?"

"Ye-yes. I'm fine. Why do you ask?"

"Your voice sounds different, and you just sniffled."

"Oh." She giggled uncomfortably. "Yeah...I'm fine. Uh...how was your day?"

"You mean after we parted ways at the bakery?"

"Yes."

"It was okay. I went by my brother's for a while and now I'm home. I just finished taking a shower. Then I called you right after."

"Oh," Gianna said. She could picture his lean muscular body in the shower. Beneath those expensive suits of his, you could just tell he was working with a body out of this world.

"What about you, Gianna? How was your evening?"

My goodness.

His voice sounded good in person, but it translated into something powerfully sexy over the phone. He wasn't even in her presence, and he had her nerves rattled.

"You there?" he asked.

"Yes. I'm here."

"Did you hear my question, Gianna?"

"No. Sorry. I was a little distracted."

"By what?"

Your sexy voice. "Um...nothing." She sniffled again. "What was your question?"

"I asked about your evening."

"Oh!" She laughed nervously and out of place. "My evening was a typical evening for me. Nothing exciting."

"No?"

"Nope."

"You and your sister didn't go out clubbing?"

Gianna laughed. "You got jokes."

"Why do you say that?"

"Because I've never stepped a foot in a club. It's not my type of fun."

"I know. I was just playing around with you."

"And how do you know it's not my thing?"

"I can tell from your mannerisms and from the way you've described yourself to me. I know it's not something you'd typically do, which leads me to my next question. What is a typical evening for Gianna, the cupcake lady, really like?"

"That's easy. Eating dinner with my sister, watching TV, doing housework—that sort of thing. Boring right?"

"Not particularly. As long as you're having a good time...doesn't really matter what I think."

Gianna sniffled again.

Ramsey grimaced. "Are your allergies bothering you?"

"No. I don't have allergy problems."

Then why do you keep sniffling? Have you been crying? He wanted to ask but decided to go with another question instead. "What side of town do you live on?"

"I live in the University City area, off of Mallard Creek Church Road. Why do you ask?"

"I'm trying to decide on a place to take you. Is Uptown too far for you to drive on a Friday night?" He would've preferred to pick her up, but he knew she wouldn't be comfortable with that.

"No. Where will you be driving from?"

"Lake Norman."

"Oh. What restaurant did you have in mind?"

"Luce."

Gianna frowned. "Hmm...never heard of it."

"It's spelled L-U-C-E. It's an Italian restaurant."

"Is it...um...like upscale?"

"Yes, Gianna. It's upscale. I want to take you someplace nice."

"So, I would need to dress up, then?"

She sounded nervous, he could tell and since she didn't date, she wouldn't know the protocol for this. This was a stretch for her. "Yes, you would need to dress up but nothing too over-the-top. A simple dress would be nice."

"What time should I meet you there?"

"Eight-thirty, but, Gianna?"

"Yes?"

"I really would like to pick you up."

"No! I mean, that's okay. It'll be better if I drove."

"I knew you would say that," he said, "But at this point, I'm just glad you agreed to meet me."

"I can't believe I agreed. My stomach is in knots just talking to you over the phone. I can't imagine what it will be like at an actual upscale restaurant."

"It'll be fine. Now, I'm going to let you get to bed. Goodnight, Gianna."

"Goodnight, Ramsey." Gianna pressed the red button on her touchscreen phone to end the call then smiled as she laid back on the bed. Even though her nerves were shot, she was looking forward to having dinner with Ramsey. But almost instantly after her head hit the pillow, she sat straight up in a state of panic. What about Gemma?

* * *

Ramsey stood up and stretched, sauntering to his office wearing a pair of gray sweatpants. Confirming his date with Gianna felt like the ultimate deal – like he'd just signed a multimillion-dollar contract. The anticipation alone had him smiling.

Sitting in the office chair, he keyed in the password to unlock the laptop then checked his emails. He skimmed through, answered a few and as he was about to exit the email, he saw the email from Felicity James. He clicked on it.

To: Ramsey St. Claire
From: Felicity James
Subject: Temporary Log-in and Password

Mr. St. Claire,

Please find your temporary log-in and password below. If you find any matches within the Wedded Bliss database, please print them out and bring them to your next appointment.

Temporary log-in: PICKY-RSC
Temporary Password: HRD2PL3AS3

Let me know if you have any questions.

Thanks,

Felicity James
Certified Matchmaker | Wedded Bliss, Inc.

———————

Ramsey smirked and shook his head at her choice of a temporary name and password, basically calling him *picky* and *hard to please* by not so subtle means. She was right. He was picky, but when you were Ramsey St. Claire, you could be that way. Successful by his own right, he worked hard to attain his wealth, and that was after losing the love of his life. It had always been a theory of his that if he had the money back then, he could've saved Leandra's life. They were young. He'd dropped out of college to take care of her and no one in his family had money like that. All he could do was take Leandra back and forth to the doctor while realizing that she wasn't getting any better. And those treatment centers – the commercials looked friendly, inviting and informative, but if you didn't have money, there was no need in wasting your time. He learned that the hard way when, out of a state of desperation, he drove Leandra to one of their facilities and was turned away.

He blinked, focusing on the email from Felicity again and decided to log onto the site. Why? He didn't know. With a date lined up with Gianna, he was certain he didn't need their services any longer. Then he thought about something Regal had said earlier – what if Gianna was one of the women listed on Wedded Bliss? Since he had access, he decided to find out for himself. He knew she wouldn't be. Besides most of the women listed on the site were nothing but gold diggers as far as he was concerned. Gianna wasn't that type of woman. She was modest, genuinely sweet, innocent and shied away from men.

Just for kicks, he typed in her name – Gianna Jacobsen – and when a profile came up, he nearly fell out of his chair. Okay, so maybe it wasn't his Gianna.

His Gianna.

"It better not be her," he said even-toned. There wasn't a picture attached to the profile, so he clicked to open it up:

Name: Gianna Jacobsen
Age: 29
Occupation: Baker
Description: Hi. I'm Gianna Jacobsen. I like to bake cupcakes. Most people think I'm weird

and by *most people* I mean men. Men think I'm weird, which is probably the reason I'm still single. I believe in love. In happily-ever-afters. In romance. I've just never experienced it for myself. I'm too busy. Who am I kidding? I'm too flaky. Okay, scratch that last part. I'm not flaky. I'm...I don't know what I am. Aren't you just *dying* to date me? Hee hee hee. Seriously, if I were you, I'd click off of this profile ASAP. Nothing to see here. I'm invisible, hence the reason I didn't upload a pic. If I were as fabulous as my bestie, I'd upload a picture, but trust me, you don't want to see this face. You wouldn't see it, anyway. No one does.

Interesting facts about me: I've had full custody of my little sister since I was 19. She's my family, all I have in this world and I love her dearly.

Anything else you want to add: It is my belief that, like life, love is fleeting in this world—here one day and gone the next. That's why you should hang on to the people you love and let them know you love them every day because they can be here today and gone tomorrow.

Ramsey must've read the profile five times over before he leaned back in his chair and frowned. He didn't know what to make of it. What was she doing on this website? It bothered him. It wasn't in her character to do something as risky as finding a date online – especially a husband. And why did her profile not seem legitimate – like she didn't want to find a man by talking down about herself, calling herself invisible, flaky and weird? A woman looking to impress a man wouldn't say those things about herself. Did she have some self-esteem issues?

That night, he couldn't sleep thinking about her being listed on the website. At two in the morning, he tossed and turned whenever he would think of her going on dates with those men who may have found her profile. How many dates had she been on? Did she find any of the men interesting? Was she seeing or dating other men currently? Is that what her *obligations* consisted of?

Chapter 9

GIANNA HAD TAKEN steps to make sure her sister was taken care of while she was gone. That way, she wouldn't feel so guilty about leaving her. She placed a bowl of soup in the microwave for easy access. She even arranged to have Felicity stop by the house to check on her. Still, she would rather be there with Gemma herself. In fact, she was having second thoughts about leaving her, but Gemma convinced her to go. Told her she needed to have some fun, too.

So, she went. After parking her Honda, she stepped out pulled in a deep breath and headed for the double glass entrance of Luce. She stepped inside, was instantly greeted by the maître D who asked for her name, then showed her to the table where Ramsey had been waiting.

Ramsey was about to take a sip of wine when he looked up and saw her. He set the glass back down on the white tablecloth and looked up at her again, his eyes widening to take in the full view of this gorgeous beauty. Wow!

He couldn't believe his eyes. As far as looks, she definitely wasn't the same woman from the bakery. Her hair – the first time he'd seen it loose was luxuriously black and tossed with curls, tumbling around her shoulders, enhancing her already beautiful face. She'd applied just a few touches of makeup, and he particularly liked the red lipstick that brought out the lovely shape of her full lips. Then there was her dress – the short black body-hugging dress that stopped mid-thigh showing off a bomb body that was ordinarily hidden behind a black apron. The neckline dipped just enough to tease his eyes. And her legs – it had to have been the sexiest pair he'd ever seen on a woman. They were smooth and buttery brown, leading down to a pair of strappy red heels that made her appear at least four inches taller. To be a man who wasn't primarily concerned with looks, he surely found himself in a daze with her. So had the other men whose heads turned when she walked by.

"Here you are, madam," the maître D said to her.

"Hi," Gianna said to Ramsey.

He had every intention of standing to get her chair, but he was so stunned, he was still seated. Then, he snapped out of it, quickly rose up from his seat and pulled out her chair.

"Thank you," she said as she sat down.

"You're welcome," Ramsey told her, getting a whiff of the perfume of whatever it was that smelled so freakin' good on the exposed portion of her back. Everything in him wanted to lower his mouth there and leave a kiss, but considering how skittish she was, she'd probably jump through the roof. No exaggeration.

"Your server will be right with you," the maître D said.

"Thank you," Ramsey told him. "Then he focused his attention on the beauty sitting across the table from him. She was pristine, yet sensual at the same time. Stunned he couldn't do anything but observe at first. When he could finally find a remnant of his voice, he said, "Hi."

"Hi." She smiled.

"You look absolutely stunning," he said, gazing into her chatoyant, light brown eyes.

A flush crept up her face. "I wouldn't take it that far, but thank you."

He stared more seeing her cheeks redden while recognizing again how hard it was for her to make eye contact with him. "Wow!"

She blushed again. "Don't do that. You're making me nervous. I mean, I'm already nervous. You're making it worse." Gianna scanned the table for water. She saw ice water in a goblet nearest to her and reached for it. Instead of picking it up, she accidentally knocked it over – water and ice spilling all over the table.

"Shoot!" she said unraveling the triangle-folded, black, cloth napkin to wipe up the mess, inadvertently pushing her utensils off the table and onto the floor. She had already attracted the attention of the guests sitting closest to them, but now, even more people were looking to see what all the noise was about.

"Here, let me," Ramsey told her.

"No. I got it," Gianna said frantically dabbing the area and picking up ice, dropping pieces back into the goblet.

"Gianna, let me get the server to clean this up. Don't worry about it, okay."

She still had the napkin in her hand trying to fix the situation when Ramsey placed his hand on top of hers to make her stop.

"It's okay," he said, looking at her. "I'll take care of it."

Gianna pulled her hand away from him. "I can't do this." She headed for the exit.

"Gianna, wait." Ramsey walked swiftly to catch up to her, but she'd already passed through the doors. As he was on the way out to find her, he informed the server that he needed a new table then he exited through the double doors. He caught up to Gianna as she descended the steps to get to the sidewalk. Latching onto her forearm with his hand, he asked, "Where are you going?"

"I'm going home," she said in full panic mode with misty eyes. Her hands trembled. "I can't do this."

"You can't do what?" he asked, his voice soft. "You can't have dinner with me?"

Her breaths were quick and forceful. Her face still flushed. She didn't respond. She wanted nothing more than to leave already. She'd embarrassed herself enough for one night.

"Gianna?"

"I—I can't, Ramsey. This is not me. This is not who I am. I don't do this. I don't know *how* to do this. I can't even sit at a table without spilling a drink like a little kid."

"It was an accident," Ramsey he said, trying to reason with her. "It's okay. I got us a new table."

"No. It's *not* okay. I—I—I feel like I'm having a pa-panic attack." She grabbed his hand and placed it on her chest. "Do you feel that? I feel like my heart is going to crack my ribcage. That's how hard it's beating. This isn't easy for me, Ramsey. I have panic attacks. This is why I didn't want to come here but I thought, for once in my life, I could try to be *normal* and go out. With a man. With a man as phenomenal as you. I thought I could but I can't."

"Gianna," Ramsey said, lowering his hand from her chest and wrapping his arms around her instead.

She looked at him.

"You *can* do this. You spilled water. So what?"

She shook her head.

"And I'm the same guy you ate dinner with at your bakery yesterday. Look at me, Gianna."

She tilted her head upwards to look at him, eyes scanning his entire face before settling on his concerned eyes.

"I'm the same guy," he said. "I don't want you to feel nervous around me, and I'll try my best to make you feel as comfortable as possible. Okay?"

She nodded. "Okay."

He lowered his arms from around her and asked, "Can we go back inside now?"

Still nervous about doing so, Gianna looked down, wanting to break away from him and make a mad dash for her car.

With the slightest touch of his index finger, Ramsey nudged her chin upward so she could look at him. "Will you please come back inside with me?"

She studied his eyes and saw the sincerity of his request deep within their depths "Yes."

He smiled. "Okay." He took her left hand into his right and that simple touch had her feeling warm all over.

After they ascended a short set of stairs, he opened the door to Luce, allowing her to enter. Then he clutched her hand once more as they followed the maître D to a new table – one that gave them more privacy.

Ramsey pulled out a chair for Gianna, and after she sat down, he sat across from her again. "Better?" he asked.

She looked across the table to see him – to *really* see him for the first time tonight. He looked sophisticated and debonair in a black suit, silver and black vest with a white shirt underneath. Either the ambiance or the suit did something to darken his eyes. Or maybe they'd darken when he would look at her. She was sure plenty of women were eyeing him. He was just that handsome. That phenomenal.

"Gianna Jacobsen?"

Her lips transformed into a beautiful smile.

"Oh. Yes, this is much better," she said. "I may need you to hold my glass for me though." She laughed.

So did he. "You'll be fine."

The server brought over the bottle of wine and poured some for Gianna. "I'll give you two a few minutes to look at the menu."

Ramsey watched Gianna as she took a sip of wine. He hoped it would help to ease her nerves a little. "I'm going to order the agnolotti. Do you know what you want?"

She glanced up at him then back at the menu. "Maybe I'll try the spaghetlini."

"Nice. You'll like that."

When the waiter came by, he took their dinner orders directly from Ramsey then walked away.

"Thank you for ordering for me," Gianna said.

"You're welcome."

"Is this usually how it works?" she asked. "The man orders for the woman?"

"That's how it works when you're with me, yes."

She took a sip of wine, glancing up to see the inquisitive glare on his face.

"Are you implying that you've never been on a date?" he asked her.

"Do you consider this a date?" she asked.

"Yes, I do."

"Oh. I um...I thought you were just wanting to share dinner with me like we did last night."

A dimple settled in his cheek. "Well, let me clarify things for you. When a man asks a woman out to dinner, he's asking her out on a date."

"Got it," she said, but still didn't have a clue

why he would want to go on a date with her.

"Now, back to my original question—have you ever been on a date, Gianna?"

"Somehow I feel like you've already asked me that before, but to answer your question, no. I don't have time to date."

Yes, he had asked her that before and thanks to the profile she had on Wedded Bliss, he felt the need to ask her again. Deciding to probe even further, he asked, "Have you ever tried online dating?"

"No."

His brows raised. "Never?"

"Nope. Never," she responded.

"What about a matchmaking service?" he asked, immediately taking a sip of wine afterward, wondering if she'd be honest about her profile on Wedded Bliss. If she wasn't upfront with him, it would tell him a lot about her. She had no reason to lie about her profile.

"No. Definitely not a matchmaking service," she replied with a chuckle. "I could never be courageous enough to do something that spontaneous."

Ramsey took a sip of wine, attempting to hide his disappointment. He had expected her to just come out and be truthful about it, but she was telling him a lie right to his face. He could still see her profile in his head. He'd read it so many times last night he had the entire thing – every word of it – committed to memory.

"Oh, you know what? I take that back," Gianna said. "The closest thing I've come to a matchmaking service is putting a profile on the website called, Wedded Bliss. Have you heard of it?"

He was relieved that she was being honest now, but still, he wanted to know why she was on that website in the first place. "I have. So, you've met some men going through that route then?" he asked, wondering why it bothered him so much to get the question out.

"No," she said amid laughter.

The food arrived before any further interrogation could ensue. Gianna sampled hers immediately. "This is good," she mumbled.

Ramsey hadn't touched his food. He didn't bother to pick up a fork, knife – nothing. He just stared at her, annoyed about her admission. If she was really the introverted woman who didn't date, why did she put a profile on Wedded Bliss?

She looked up at him and slowly stopped chewing when she realized he wasn't eating. He was just staring at her. "What?" she asked, hiding her mouth with her hand.

"I was just thinking—if you've never met or dated anyone from Wedded Bliss, why did you put a profile on the site? Were you looking for a husband?"

"No. I wasn't looking for a husband. I did it as a favor."

"A favor to who?"

"To my best friend." She smiled. "You may find this hard to believe but the woman who owns Wedded Bliss, Felicity James, is my best friend. We've been friends since fifth grade. Anyway, she's a big dreamer with an even bigger personality—waaay bigger than mine and she got the idea to start the company when she was in college. When she had the website built, she asked me to enter a profile to test out the system before she rolled it out. After everything tested successfully, she inactivated my profile."

A smile appeared on his face then grew as relief settled him. He picked up his fork. He couldn't believe Felicity and Gianna knew each other and that they were best friends, especially with their completely opposite personalities. But most of all, he was relieved that Gianna was telling him the truth. Now, things were starting to make sense.

"How's your food?" she asked him.

"Good. Hey, last night when we talked, you seemed upset."

"I was fine," she said.

"No. You were upset. Tell me why."

She looked up narrowing her eyes at him. "Why do you think I was upset?"

"Because you were sniffling, and when you confirmed you didn't have allergies, I knew you'd been crying. Tell me why."

She instantly clammed up. She wasn't comfortable discussing details about Gemma's sickness with him. "I'd rather not talk about it."

"Okay," he said, hiding his annoyance. He didn't like how she was withholding information from him, but he couldn't *make* her talk. Still, it irritated him. He swished wine around in the glass while asking, "What does Gemma do for a living?"

Gianna grimaced. "She doesn't work."

"Right. She's nineteen. Is she in college?"

"No. What about your brother—the one you went to visit yesterday? What does he do?"

"His name is Regal, by the way. He's also an architect with St. Claire Architects. My other brothers, Royal and Romulus also works with us. Royal is the youngest, a pain in my rear, and he's the troubleshooter—go figure. Romulus is our land finder."

"That's wonderful. Keeping it all in the family," she said.

"Have you ever been in love, Gianna?"

"No. Have you?"

"Yes. Once."

"What happened to end the relationship?" she inquired.

"She passed away."

"Oh. Sorry to hear that."

Ramsey lowered his fork to the white ceramic plate, dabbed the corners of his mouth with the napkin, then asked, "Do you believe in love?"

"Yes."

"You've just never been in it?"

"That's correct," she said.

"What about your parents? Are they still together?"

Goodness. He was hitting her with back-to-back questions. She took a breath. "You sure ask a lot of questions."

"How else am I supposed to get to know

you?" *How else do I get to the bottom of why I'm so taken by you? So drawn to you?* Ramsey studied her, watching her grow uneasy.

"If we see each other beyond this one *date*, maybe I'll tell you about my family. Until then can we just stick to generic topics?"

"You mean, meaningless topics," he said examining her.

She locked eyes with his dark ones. "No. That's not what I meant." She thought for a moment and decided to turn the tables with questions of her own. "What do you do outside of work?"

He exhaled noisily. "Sometimes, I play golf with my brother, Regal. I don't really have much of a life outside of my work."

"Do you date?" she asked using her fork to push spaghetti around her plate.

"I do. Sometimes. This is the first date I've been on in roughly six years."

Gianna giggled. "I *know* you don't expect me to believe that!" She watched his expression grow more intense.

Instead of answering, Ramsey picked up his glass and finished off the rest of his wine in one small gulp. He set the glass on the table and twirled the stem.

"Okay, he's serious Gianna. Stop insulting the man."

A grin settled in the corner of his lips. "You're talking out loud again. You do realize that right?"

She hid her face behind her hands. "I suck at this. I know. I can't even make an excuse for myself. I'm horrible."

He chuckled. "You're not horrible."

"I am."

"Why don't you believe me when I say I haven't been on a date in six years?"

"Because honestly, you are handsome and dreamy and accomplished. I imagine women must throw themselves at you."

"I get that kind of attention from women, but that's not what I'm looking for. I like a woman who's interesting. Who keeps me guessing. A woman with ambition—not a woman who only has a body to offer. Frankly speaking, I can get a body from anywhere. I want a heart. A soul."

"Oh."

"What about you? What do you want in a man, Gianna?"

She shrugged. "I don't know. I haven't given it much thought."

He grinned a little to cover his building dissatisfaction with her lack of communication skills. "I need you to be a little more open than that."

"I'm telling you the truth. I haven't—"

"Tell me what's in your heart," he broke in to say.

Gianna sighed heavily. Why did he want to get so deep on the first date?

Trying another approach, Ramsey said, "Look...think of me as one of your girlfriends, okay, and we're having a discussion about men and I ask you to tell me what qualities you find appealing in a man. What would you say?"

"Honesty, for one," she answered. "That's a good quality."

Ramsey sat back in his chair. That's not the answer he was seeking but what else did he expect after she already admitted that she didn't date? This was awkward for her and frustrating for him since he was wanting more than what she was able to give.

"Do you think you're going to want some dessert?" he asked her.

"No. I'm stuffed," she said. She wasn't an expert when it came to this, but if he was asking about dessert, he must've been ready to go.

"I'll get the check when the server comes back. Okay?"

She was right. "Okay."

After Ramsey paid the check, they walked outside. It was dark now, but the city was just coming alive. Traffic on Tryon Street was bumper to bumper. The sidewalks were filled with people going this way and that way. To clubs. Bars. Restaurants. The EpiCentre.

And here they were about to go their separate ways when the night was still so young. Ramsey had high hopes that time alone with her would get her to open up to him, but that didn't happen. "Gianna, where'd you park?" he asked.

"A few blocks away."

"Come on. I'll walk with you."

"That's okay. I can make it there on my own. Thanks for dinner." She glanced up at him, watching him frown, but didn't say anything in response. She took a few steps away before she could embarrass herself anymore tonight, but after a few strides of his long legs, he caught up to her. She glanced over at him. He had his hands in his pockets while looking straight ahead, keeping up with her steps. He made no effort to hold her hand like he'd done before. Whatever kind of *date* this was, she knew she had officially blown it. A part of her felt relieved that she wouldn't have to worry about ever seeing him again – popping up at her bakery out of the blue, intimidating her with his overbearing presence. But that very same feeling was also the reason she felt a level of sadness. Ramsey was a distraction from the norm for her. Men didn't give her attention. Open doors for her. Go out of their way to make her talk. Ask her out on dates at fancy restaurants. Make goosebumps run up and down her body with just eye contact alone. But this one did. Now, she wouldn't have that exciting feeling of what if. What if the weird, miserable baker had a life with a man like Ramsey St. Claire?

She sighed as they got closer to her car. Who was she kidding? Men like Ramsey didn't end up with ditzy cupcake bakers. It was never something that was meant to be. It was just a date. One date. And she didn't make a good impression on him. There were several times when he seemed frustrated. Even now, he wasn't saying anything. Just walking.

"It's one more block up," she said breaking the silence between them as they walked along.

"Sorry you had to walk so far," he said.

"It's not a problem," Gianna said. *I'm sorry our date was horrible.*

"Did you enjoy your meal?" he asked.

She turned to catch a glimpse of him. "Yes, I did."

Finally, they were approaching her car. She unlocked the door. He opened it for her. There was no parting hug. No dreamy, first-date kiss, not that she was expecting one. She'd probably turn into a pile of sugar if Ramsey's lips ever touched hers.

"Thanks," she said, getting inside, adjusting her dress after she put her purse on the front passenger seat.

"You're welcome. Drive safe on your way home," he said.

"I will. Thanks."

With that he, he expelled a long breath and closed the door.

Gianna started the car and checked the mirrors as she pulled out of the parking space and onto the street. Then the self-badgering began. "I'm such a freaking nut case," she said, talking to herself. "I should've said, no. I shouldn't have gone on the date. Now...now he thinks I'm a complete moron. Why can't I just be normal? Ugh!"

Thinking that her sister was asleep by now, she called Felicity to find out how Gemma was doing.

"Hello?" Felicity answered, wondering why Gianna was calling her.

"Hey, how's Gem?"

"Gemma's asleep," Felicity told her. "Now get off of this phone and go enjoy your date, girl."

"There's nothing left to enjoy. I'm actually on my way back home."

"Already?"

"Yes. I just left the restaurant."

"But it's still early."

"It's 10:23 p.m. That's late by my standards. Anyway, I should be there in about twenty minutes, so feel free to go on home."

"No, ma'am," Felicity said. "I want to hear all the details. Get ready to spill the beans when you get here missy."

"Felicity, please don't make me relive the night."

"Every. Single. Detail. I'll be waiting. Love you. Drive safe. Bye, chica."

Gianna dropped her phone on the passenger seat when Felicity ended the call. Her stomach cinched when she thought about how horrible the night had gone with Ramsey and now she had to relay the story to her best friend.

Chapter 10

SHE PARKED AND walked to her own house feeling like a sore loser. After letting herself in, she dropped her purse on the table in the foyer and met Felicity's curious stare.

"Don't hit me with back-to-back questions. I've answered enough of those already tonight."

"Just tell me how it went," Felicity said. "Wait, first, tell me the man's name, girlfriend so I can visualize him."

Gianna shook her head. "You don't need to know his name or visualize him because I'm never going to see him again. Okay."

"Whatever. Where did y'all go?"

Gianna fell on the sofa and kicked off her heels. "We went to Luce."

"Ooh...good choice. That's the kind of place a man takes you when he wants to propose."

"Well, trust me when I say there is *no* proposal in my future. Not from him or anybody else. I wouldn't know what to do with a man in my life, anyway."

"Uh, yes you do and you desperately need to *do it*." Felicity laughed.

"Whatever Felicity. Anyway, the dinner was a complete catastrophe. When I arrived, he was already there staring at me so hard as I approached the table, I could hardly breathe. But, he was a complete gentleman. He pulled out my chair. I sat down with my nerves already fried. So, I reached for my water goblet and in true Gianna fashion, I knocked it over instead. Water and ice spilled everywhere."

"Oh, no," Felicity said.

"But wait...there's more. It was at this point that I had a full-on panic attack, told him I couldn't do it—*it* being the date—and sprinted out of the restaurant."

Felicity covered her mouth. "No you did not!"

"I did. It gets worse. He followed me outside, convinced me to come *back* inside after I'd made a complete fool of myself and we resumed dinner. Then the questions started. He wanted to know a bunch of personal things about me. Wanted to know about Gemma. I told him I wanted to keep our discussions about generic topics. He seemed irritated by that."

"You're supposed to open up a lil' bit on the first date, Gianna. I knew I should've schooled you before you went out with that man."

"Trust me, it would've been for nothing. You can't fix me. I am the way I am."

"Keep talking like that and you'll die a virgin."

Gianna darted her tongue out at her friend. "I'd already planned on it."

Felicity chuckled.

"Get this," Gianna went on to say. "He told me he hadn't been on a date in six years and I pretty much called him a liar to his face."

"You didn't believe him?"

"No. The man is incredibly hot, Felicity. He's the epitome of what a man should be. I know he gets a lot of attention from women. Why would I believe he hadn't been on a date in six years?"

"Hello. You're pretty smokin' hot yourself and this was your first date *ever*."

"It wasn't a date."

"Oh, please it was a date."

"Well, whatever it was there surely won't be another. There. End of story."

Felicity shook her head. "That's just what you wanted, too isn't it?"

"Felicity don't start with me."

"Somebody needs to. Gosh, you've been doing this for how long?"

Gianna stood up and said, "What? Taking care of my sister? Of my responsibilities?"

Gianna walked into the kitchen and took a bottle of water from the refrigerator.

Hot on her trail, Felicity said, "You know what I mean. You have a way of sabotaging any chance of happiness that comes your way. How long are you going to keep living this way?"

"What do you want me to do, Felicity? What choice do I have? Gemma is my sister. I'm her caregiver. I take care of her. I work every day for her." Her eyes teared up. "I bust my butt every single day and take every dime I have just to pay for her treatment. I don't have time for anything or anyone else."

Felicity walked over to her friend and

wrapped her arms around her. "You know I love you, Gianna."

"I know."

"I just want you to be happy. You've given up so much. You deserve some happiness, too."

"Trust me. I've had these in-depth conversations with God. He knows I can't take much more," she said tearfully.

Felicity released her and said, "I'll be at the bakery to help you out tomorrow."

"No, Felicity. Don't give up your Saturday for me. I'll be fine."

"No. Saturday is your busiest day. I'm going to help you. Okay?"

"Okay."

"Let me go so I can rest up. See you in the morning, doll."

Gianna pinched tears away from her eyes and said, "Okay."

Chapter 11

RAMSEY SWUNG THE nine iron and whacked the golf ball so hard, he could've cracked it open.

"You cool?" Regal asked with one eyebrow arched up.

"Yeah. I'm cool," Ramsey grumbled.

"Are you sure about that?"

Ramsey whacked another. "Yeah. I'm fine," he said, striking yet another one with all his might.

"A'ight. Timeout. Let's take a break. You obviously need one."

Ramsey dropped his club in the bag and walked with Regal to the Country Club's clubhouse. He fixed up a cup of coffee then sat in a lounge chair. He took a sip and glanced up at the investigative eyes of his brother.

"Go on. Get it off your chest, man," Regal said.

"It's...nothing."

"It's this woman isn't it?"

Ramsey frowned.

"What happened?" Regal asked.

"I asked her out to dinner."

"And what? She shot you down?"

"No. It took a lot of coaxing on my part, but

she accepted. However, it didn't go as smoothly as I'd hoped."

"Let me guess...she's already involved with someone."

"No, she's not."

"Then?"

Ramsey set his coffee cup on the table. "She won't let me in."

Regal chuckled. "You just met her and you're already trying to get *in*?"

"I'm not talking about sex, Regal."

"I know. I'm just messing with you, Ram."

"Well, I'm not in the mood for games. If you want to give me advice, give me advice."

"Okay," Regal said. "You're serious."

"Yes, I'm serious. I really like this woman."

"I see that. You have to give me a while to process this new you. I never thought I'd see the day when my big brother would fall for a complete stranger after fifteen years of avoiding anything close to a real relationship."

Ramsey rubbed his hands across his head.

"So, what happened? Dinner didn't go smoothly, you said."

"No, it didn't. Gianna was a nervous wreck, but I expected that so it wasn't much of a problem for me. The problem is, she only wanted to keep our conversations on the surface. I wanted to delve deeper. I wanted to know her family, her motivation for running a bakery—I wanted to know everything."

Regal lifted a brow. "On the first date?"

"Yes. I know it sounds crazy, but yes I wanted to know it all."

"Do you think that's fair to her? To completely offload her life on someone she just met?"

"No, I don't. Typically I wouldn't ask that of anyone but *this* woman..."

Regal sat up and stared at his brother for a moment. Ramsey was truly in anguish. "Gianna must be some woman."

A smile came to Ramsey's face. "She is," Ramsey said, thinking about her. He hated how last night ended, and he got the vibe from her that she was glad the date was over especially since she had been uneasy from the get-go.

"Tell me about her."

His eyes darted up at his brother. "Seriously?"

"Yes, seriously. I know when you're not in a joking mood and I also know you haven't been on a date in like fifteen years."

"Six years," Ramsey clarified.

"My bad," Regal said. The fifteen-year span was the time that had passed since Leandra had died. "Okay, six. There must be something special about this particular woman. Tell me."

Ramsey shuffled through his thoughts. "She's refreshing. Honest. She always smells sweet. When I look into her eyes, whenever she gives me the opportunity to do so, I see things she won't tell me." He looked up at his brother. "You know how when women meet us and they're trying hard to be pretty and impressive just to get our attention because of who we are?"

"All too well my brother."

"And when you look at them, all you see is a body. No soul. You look into their eyes and nothing's there."

Regal bunched up his eyebrows. "I think I get what you're trying to say."

"In contrast, when I look into Gianna's eyes, I see pain. I see hurt and anguish. Disappointment. Even beyond her smiles—beyond her frazzled nerves, I can see it. That's what I wanted to know. I wanted to know the source of that pain. I know I have no right to know, but I feel like I can be selfish this time. I want to know."

"You're attracted to her pain?"

"No. I'm attracted to her heart—the place where she's holding the pain. I told you something is pulling me toward her and I—I can't let go. Even after last night." He rubbed his hand across his mustache.

"And you've never felt anything like this before?"

"No. Never."

"What does she do again?"

"She owns a bakery. She makes cupcakes—all varieties."

"How do you know that? I told you...that's where I met her. I walked into her bakery one day."

"Right...which still has me thrown considering you don't eat sweets. Why would a person who hates sweets step foot into a bakery?"

"Good question, isn't it?" Ramsey asked. "I was there because I was *supposed* to meet her.

When I walked in, she was on her cell phone with her butt pressed up against the counter. She had no idea whatsoever that I was standing behind her and when she turned around, she literally screamed. I scared the living daylights out of her." He chuckled, remembering.

Regal looked at Ramsey like he was nuts. Maybe working so many years at the firm had finally taken a toll on him. Mentally. "So, you got a cupcake that day?"

"A butter pecan cupcake that was absolutely delicious. I ate the cupcake and drank coffee while I watched her work. I was the only customer, at the time, until this homeless man showed up. She gave him a half dozen cupcakes. For free." Ramsey took a sip of coffee then placed the cup back on the table. "But we're getting off track here. My point is, I *need* to know her. I need to know the source of her sadness. I need to know why she put on this façade of happiness when I can see and feel the sadness when I'm with her."

"What if she doesn't want to talk about it? This ain't a *Wedded Bliss* situation where women agree to marry you and get to know you after the fact—a concept that I think is absolutely asinine to begin with—"

"She's on the site," Ramsey blurted out.

Regal looked puzzled. "Gianna is on Wedded Bliss?"

"When you asked me if she was on there, I went home and checked, and sure enough her profile appeared, but there was no picture…just information about her. Without giving myself away, I did manage to find out over dinner that she's on the site because her best friend, Felicity James, owns Wedded Bliss and had Gianna enter a profile for testing purposes. The only thing is, her friend forgot to deactivate Gianna's fake account."

Regal squeezed his eyes and opened them wide. "My mind is officially blown. How does this stuff only happen to you man?"

Ramsey smirked.

"Think about it—you have all the pieces you need to end your obsession with this girl."

"How so?"

"When is your next appointment at Wedded Bliss?"

"I told Felicity I'd get back to her on Monday."

Regal scooted to the edge of his seat. "Check this out—you already know the owner is Gianna's best friend, right?"

"Correct."

"Does Gianna know you're affiliated with Wedded Bliss in any way?"

"No, and she has no idea I know Felicity."

"And what about Felicity? Does she know that you know Gianna?"

Ramsey shrugged. "I don't know. My guess would be no. I have to imagine if she did, she would've said something to me by now. Felicity is not the kind of woman to bite her tongue."

"Then, there you have it. Get Felicity to tell you everything you need to know about Gianna."

Ramsey chuckled. "I can't do that."

"Why not, Ram? It's brilliant. Once you talk to Felicity and find out everything you need to know about Gianna, you won't find her so mysterious and interesting. Then, your life can go back to normal."

"Normal, meaning working myself into an early grave?"

"But you *love* working."

"Yes, because I have nothing else. Nothing." Ramsey stood up and quietly paced the floor near the area where they were sitting – where Regal still sat. "There has to be more out there for me, Regal."

"What more do you need? You have everything—no, you have the *best* of everything. Take the firm for example. You built that from the ground up—no pun intended."

Ramsey smirked. "Give yourself some credit, too. You were right there with me."

"True, but it was your vision, Ram. You went from a home office making thousands, which was impressive on its own merits, to a ten-floor building of employees where you make millions. You own houses, cars, a yacht—there is nothing you don't have."

"I don't have love. I don't have anyone to share my accomplishments with."

"You said you didn't want love," Regal reminded him.

"I know what I said."

"You said Leandra was your soulmate and there was no reason to look for anyone else after she died because no one could compare to her. Everyone in our family knew your stance when it came to Leandra. That's why, to this day, mom and dad will never mention anything to you about meeting someone, getting married and having a family. Not a thing. But every time they see me, Romulus and Royal, that's all they talk about, well especially mom because she knows that her oldest son gave up on those things since losing the love of his life."

Regal took a breath and then continued, "I'm not stupid. I know that's precisely the reason you wanted to join Wedded Bliss. You were hoping to get married quickly just to have some companionship—some form of normality in your life—and you needed to do that with a woman you knew you could never love because no woman can be Leandra."

"Are you done?" Ramsey asked, eyebrows raised. "You're right. Everything you said is true. I poured myself into work because I have nothing else. Losing Leandra broke my spirit, and you don't know how incredibly painful that is, Regal, because you haven't lived it. I don't have everything. I want to love again."

"You want to love, but are you truly capable of loving somebody or is every woman you attempt to love *not* going to measure up to who you were with Leandra?"

"I don't know. I don't know that. I can't predict how I will feel in the future about someone I don't even know. What I do know is, it's been fifteen years and I think I'm finally ready to find out. No, I *know* I'm ready because I've finally had a true connection with someone."

"With Gianna?"

"Yes."

"The shy cupcake girl."

Ramsey smiled. "Yes. The shy cupcake girl and I want to explore that connection. I want to find out why I'm drawn to her...why I can't stop thinking about her."

"How are you going to go about doing that?"

"That much, I haven't quite figured out yet."

"Does the bakery open on Saturdays?"

"It does."

"Then, go see her."

"No. I'm sure she needs breathing room after our not-so-good date last night. Maybe I'll call her. I don't know yet."

Regal smiled. "I'm proud of you man."

Ramsey chuckled. "Why?"

"For trying again. I know it took a lot out of you."

"You have no idea," Ramsey said. "Hey and keep this between us for now. I don't want to get the folks all worked up."

"Not a problem, man."

Chapter 12

LATE IN THE afternoon, when he knew it would be near closing time for the bakery, Ramsey parked across the street in front of the Vietnamese restaurant. He strode over the boardwalk bridge, passed the boat rental and looked into the window of the bakery where he saw Gianna standing behind the counter with another woman he recognized – Felicity James – her best friend. A small grin touched his lips. He had no reason to doubt that Gianna was being truthful when she told him Felicity was her best friend, but this confirmed it. He wondered if Gianna had told Felicity about him, in turn prompting Felicity to tell Gianna that he was a client of hers at Wedded Bliss. And if she had told her, how did Gianna feel about it?

Peering through the window again, focusing strictly on Gianna this time, he watched her smile as she interacted with a customer. Her smile made him smile, just like that. And it was instant. *Goodness*. He had it bad.

He wanted to see her up close, not through a window, but he couldn't right now – not with Felicity there. He didn't exactly have a good rapport with Felicity and he definitely didn't need the negative energy he felt whenever he had to interact with her regarding Wedded Bliss. So, he walked away, heading back for his car when he heard the voice of a man say, "Hey, I know you."

Ramsey glanced around and found the source of the voice – the homeless man, Jerry, that he recognized from the bakery. He was sitting on the sidewalk near some bushes and an area where skateboarders frequented even though skateboarding wasn't allowed at the boardwalk.

Waving his index finger, Jerry said, "Yeah, that's it. I saw you in the bakery."

"Yes, you did. Your name is Jerry, right?"

"Yes, *suh*. Pleased to meet your acquaintance Mr.?"

"St. Claire," Ramsey said, reaching down to shake the man's hand. He remembered Gianna said she'd known Jerry for two years. He wondered just how much Jerry knew about her.

"Hey, Jerry, I was just about to grab some dinner at Boardwalk Billy's. Would you like to join me?"

"I'm afraid I don't have money for dinner," the man said.

"No problem. I got it covered."

The man's eyes shot open wide. "You-you said you got it covered?"

"Yes. It's on me."

"Well, all right, then." Jerry struggled to get up off of the sidewalk.

Ramsey leaned forward, clutched his hand

and helped pull him up. "Thank you," Jerry said.

"No problem."

They walked back across the wooden bridge to get to Boardwalk Billy's – one of the most popular restaurants at the boardwalk – that served pretty much anything you could want, from oysters to jerk chicken. Stepping inside, they were immediately greeted by a hostess who led them to a table near the bar.

The place smelled like barbecue – like somebody was having a backyard cookout. When they settled at the table, Ramsey looked at Jerry and asked, "Have you eaten here before?"

"No. You can't eat at places like this when you're broke." Jerry chuckled, sounding rough and gritty.

When the waitress showed up, Ramsey ordered grilled shrimp tacos and Jerry opted for a Philly cheese steak and fries.

While they waited for the food, Jerry said, "Hey, man...those cupcakes are addictive aren't they?"

Ramsey smiled. He was addicted to a whole lot more than just the cupcakes.

"She's a good lady, I tell you. A good lady. I remember when she first opened. I thought she was going to run me off. Imagine my surprise when she brought me a cupcake instead." Jerry chuckled. "I said to myself, what is this pretty young thang doing taking an interest in me? I was baffled. Still am to this day. She gives me cupcakes for free, and I feel mighty bad that I can't pay her for them. Mighty bad."

"Why?" Ramsey asked.

"Well, for the same reason I feel bad about you buying me a meal. I'm a man. A man is supposed to be able to stand on his own two feet—not take handouts."

"Well, sometimes we need help."

Jerry looked up at Ramsey. "And when was the last time you needed help, Mr. St. Claire?"

Ramsey couldn't recall the last time he needed help with anything.

"See my point," Jerry said.

"What's so bad about her giving you a few cupcakes here and there if she's doing so out of the kindness of her heart?"

"She...um...nevermind. It ain't my place to be telling folks business."

"No, tell me. I want to know your reasoning on this."

"Well, um...her sister has taken a turn for the worst. Honestly, when I go into that bakery, I'm not looking for her to give me cupcakes, St. Claire. I'm just making sure she's okay, and I think she knows that. In turn, she pays me with cupcakes."

Ramsey's heart thudded in his chest. "Wait— what do you mean her sister has taken a turn for the worst?"

"Cancer. Her sister has lung cancer—never smoked a day in her life but the poor thing has cancer."

Jerry's words nearly knocked the air right out of Ramsey. Cancer? Gianna's sister had lung cancer? Cancer was the disease that took the love of his life away. Lung cancer to be exact. Cancer was the plague that ruined his life, and this is that exact same thing Gianna was dealing with? Now, he understood what her *obligations* entailed. She was taking care of her ill sister.

"You okay, St. Claire?"

Ramsey looked up at Jerry. "I'm—I'm fine. How do you know about Gianna's sister?"

"She told me one day when I stopped by the bakery…I'll say about a month ago now. I found her sitting on the floor crying like it was the end of the world. And she had a look in her eyes, one I'll never forget. It was a look like it was over…scared me. I asked her what was the matter. That's when she told me the cancer was out of remission. Said the doctor gave her sister two months to live and she couldn't let her sister die. Then she cried, told me she put up her house, took out some loans, every dime she makes from the bakery she uses to cover her sister's cancer treatments. That's why I feel bad about her just giving me free cupcakes, but I take them because I don't want to be rude. And, the girl makes some good cupcakes." Jerry smiled. "I just wish there was something I could do to help her, but I can't even help myself, St. Claire. How am I supposed to help *her* when I can't help *myself*?"

Ramsey's mind flooded over with replaying the last few days of his interaction with Gianna. Okay, so she didn't know him well enough to share her woes and concerns but now he knew them. Now, he understood his connection to her. He knew what led him to her—why he ended up going into the bakery that day. She needed him. Her nineteen-year-old sister was dying of cancer the same way his fiancée Leandra had passed of the same dreadful disease. He closed his eyes for a moment before he stood up and said, "I'll be right back, Jerry."

Ramsey walked to the bathroom, ran some cold water, caught some in his hands and dashed it onto his face. He couldn't believe this was happening to him. Couldn't believe the force pulling him to Gianna wasn't some meaningless, serendipitous type of happening, but it was actually a calling. He was *supposed* to meet Gianna. Having gone through the same torment she was about to go through, he knew what it would take to help her heal. And that's what he was intent on doing – helping her.

After taking a paper towel from the dispenser, he patted his face dry and exited the bathroom. Heading back to the table in hopes of finding out what else he could get out of Jerry, he frowned when he saw that the man was gone. He glanced around the restaurant looking for him, but he was nowhere in sight. Then he looked at the table where they'd been sitting and saw a note written on a napkin in barely legible handwriting: *God bless you.*

"Here you go," the waitress said handing him a takeout bag.

"What's this?" Ramsey asked.

"Oh, the man you were with said you all were taking your food to go. I gave him his already. Here's yours."

Honestly, Ramsey had forgotten all about the food. He definitely didn't have an appetite. He took out his wallet and handed the waitress a fifty-dollar bill. "That should be enough to cover the bill and tip."

"It sure is. Thank you!"

"You're welcome." Ramsey took the plastic bag and headed out of the restaurant. Outside, in the heat of a North Carolina summer afternoon, he looked around for Jerry. He even checked the area of the sidewalk where he'd first saw him. He wasn't there either.

Walking back over to the bakery, he saw the lights off now. Looking around the corner, he saw that Gianna's car was gone. Walking back to his car, he remembered the things Jerry told him. It only made him want to see her again, but since her bakery didn't open on Sundays, he didn't know how to make that happen. If he called Gianna, she would probably be too embarrassed to answer.

He frowned, thought some more. "I need to see you, Gianna," he said talking to himself. "I need to see you."

Chapter 13

"COME ON SIS. I want you to enjoy some of this sunshine today."

"Nooo," Gemma drawled out.

"Yes. A little Vitamin D ain't never hurt nobody. You've been cooped up in this house all day. Let's go sit on the porch. Come on," Gianna said, pulling the covers off of Gemma.

When Gemma's feet were safely on the floor, Gianna helped her stand up and they slowly walked to the porch.

"Nice," Gemma said as soon as the warm heat from the sun struck her face. "I love summer."

"Me too," Gianna said, trying her best to keep the sadness out of her voice, realizing that this was probably the last summer she would share with Gemma. She stopped walking when Gemma was in front of a chair. Carefully, she helped her sit there, then pulled another chair close to where Gemma was sitting.

"Felicity came by the bakery today," Gianna said. "She stayed all day, too."

"That's nice. She's a good friend."

"She is."

"You never told me how—" Gemma coughed. "How your date went."

"It wasn't a date."

"It was," Gemma said.

"Yeah, more like a pity date. There's no way a man like him would be interested in me. Things like that just don't happen to people in real life. In movies, yeah, but not in Charlotte, North Carolina."

"Oh, whatever. You're beautiful, Gianna, and you looked so pretty in that black dress you had on."

"Thank you, Gem."

Gemma smiled, looking up into the sky. "So, how was it?"

"It wasn't as good as it could have been and that's my fault."

"Why? What did you do?"

"I knocked over some water, and you know how difficult it is for me to hold conversations with people I don't know."

"But you must like this guy. You've never gone out with anyone and you've been asked plenty of times."

"Not true."

"Un huh. What about the guy from the beach last summer?"

Gianna giggled. "Okay, one guy from the beach asking me out doesn't mean I get asked out *all the time.*"

"Why did you go this time?"

"Because I did *kinda* like him."

"I knew it!" Gemma said. "What's his name?"

"Ramsey," Gemma repeated. "With a name like Ramsey he has to be handsome."

Gianna smiled. "He is."

"So you're not going to see him again?"

"Probably not."

"Aw…"

"Hey, it's no biggie. Besides, that means I'll have more time to spend with my little sister. Gianna looked at Gemma and said, "I know Dr. Willoughby gave you two months."

"How do you know that? Did he tell you because I told him not to—"

"It doesn't matter how I know. I know."

Gemma sighed heavily. "He said the chemo could buy me more time. On Monday he'll let me know if it's worth doing again."

Gianna nodded and fought back tears. Her sister needed her strong. Not weak. She cleared her throat and said, "Hey, um, I have to go grocery shopping tomorrow. Is there anything you needed in particular?"

"You mean besides soup and crackers?"

"Yes."

"I could use some cough drops."

"Okay. I'll add it to the list. Also, your doctor said you should try to eat as healthy as possible, so I'll be loading up on carrots, blueberries, apples—"

"Yeah, yeah, yeah."

After a few passing, quiet moments, Gemma said, "I think you should see him again."

"Who? Ramsey?"

"No, the mailman. Yes, Ramsey!" Gemma quipped.

"Why?"

"Because if he was interesting enough to

make you say *yes* to a date, then there must be something awesome about this guy."

"Like I said, sis...I doubt very seriously he would want to go out with me again. He hasn't called me, and if he did call, I probably wouldn't answer the phone. That's the messed up part about all of this."

"Well, I'm proud of you for going. It'll make it easier for the next guy who asks you out."

"If you say so," Gianna said, standing. "Come on let's get you back inside."

Chapter 14

LEAVE IT UP to Regal to forget to bring salad dressing...

On the way to his parent's home for Sunday dinner, Ramsey was given the task of picking up some ranch dressing since everyone had arrived but him. He figured he could stop by Trader Joe's since it was the closest grocery store to his parent's house but as he approached the Harris Teeter on University City Boulevard, he made a quick decision to stop there instead. As soon as he walked inside, her presence grabbed at him – Gianna's presence – and he knew without yet laying eyes on her that she was somewhere inside of this store. He looked around, searching for her and boom – there she was at checkout waiting to pay for her groceries. She didn't see him. He was sure of it. So, he quickly found a bottle of ranch dressing and instead of breezing through self-checkout, he stood in her line, three customers back, even after one of the store's employees informed him that there was no waiting at self-checkout. He watched Gianna swipe her credit card.

"Um, try it again," the clerk said.

"Okay," Gianna said taking the credit card

from her wallet and swiping it again. For the second time, it didn't go through.

"Do you have another card you can use?" the clerk asked her. "Or maybe cash?"

"No. Let me just try it again," Gianna said, knowing the chances of the card going through were slim especially since she hadn't paid the bill in two months.

The people in line behind her were growing impatient, already looking around for a shorter line, or perhaps a line that was moving.

Ramsey frowned, watching Gianna swipe her credit card for the third time, and still, it didn't go through. He'd seen enough.

"Excuse me," he said to the customers in front of him. He placed the ranch dressing on the candy bar rack and took out his wallet.

"Ramsey?" Gianna frowned staring at him to make sure this was really real and she was not imagining things. It was real. "Ramsey, what are you doing here?"

He took out a black credit card, swiped it and said discreetly, "I'm doing you a favor."

The clerk handed Ramsey the receipt then he took it upon himself to place her grocery bags in the cart. All packed up and ready to go, he said, "After you."

He pushed the cart while she, still in a daze, walked to her car. She opened the trunk and said, "I'm going to pay you back. Thank you. I got it from here."

Ignoring her, Ramsey picked up bags and began placing them inside of her car.

"Ramsey, I got it."

"Let me help you."

Already embarrassed – first from their botched date and now from him witnessing her inability to afford groceries – she wanted to get away from him as soon as she could. She could only imagine what he must have been thinking – how was it possible that a woman who owned her own business couldn't afford to buy groceries or better yet pay her credit card bill?

"Ramsey, I got it, okay. I can put my own bags in the car."

He was about to grab two more bags when he stopped, looked at her and said, "Let...me...help...you." He resumed picking up the bags.

"You've done enough," she said attempting to yank a bag out of his hand.

Ramsey released the bag and grabbed her instead, holding her securely in his arms while watching her lips tremble – lips he wanted to kiss until she had no more worries. Resisting the urge to do so for now, he stared into her misty, troubled eyes and said, "I want to help you. Please, let me."

A tear fell from her eye and Ramsey twitched in pain like someone had stabbed him with a knife. When he was able to shake the pain away, he thumbed the tear away and said, "Here's what I'm going to do. I'm going to finish putting these bags in the car for you. I'm going to push the cart over there to the cart return and I'm going to follow you home and help you unload it all. Okay?"

Gianna nodded. Her lips were still

trembling. When she felt his hands loosen their grip on her arm, she got inside of her car and waited for him to finish placing her groceries inside. Her eyes followed him to the cart return, then she watched him get inside of a different car – a white Range Rover this time – and drive her way. He flicked his lights signaling her to back out and she did. Then he began following her every turn.

Ramsey pushed the phone button on the steering wheel of his SUV. When prompted to say a command, he said, "Call, Regal St. Claire."

Within a few seconds, he heard the phone ringing. Then Regal's voice came through the speakers, "Hey, does it take all day to get ranch dressing?"

"Regal, something came up. I'm not going to make it."

"Oh, that's how you're going to do us?" Regal asked.

Ramsey could hear him telling the others that he wasn't going to make it.

"Tell mom I'll make it up to her," he said. "I have to go. Later." He pressed the button on his steering wheel to end the call, closely following behind Gianna. She made a left onto John Kirk Drive and once they reached the end of that street, she made another left onto Mallard Creek Church Road. Traveling that road, she crossed over Tryon Street and continued over the I-85 overpass. Shortly thereafter, she made a right on Senator Royall Drive and another right on Arbor Vista Drive. After passing a few houses, she pulled into the driveway of a two-story home. He pulled up behind her and got out of the Range.

Walking to her car, he grabbed a handful of bags and she carried them with her left hand. She kept her right hand free so she could unlock the door. So, why was she having a problem getting the door unlocked? Probably because she had a hot guy towering over her shoulder with grocery bags. In addition to that, she was nervous about him seeing Gemma and asking a flurry of questions.

"Do you need me to get that?" he asked.

"No. I can get it. It's my nerves. One sec."

When she was able to hold the keys steady, she finally unlocked the door.

Ramsey followed her to the kitchen. "Where do you want me to put the bags?"

"Just...um...set them on the counter."

"Okay," he said lowering the bags wherever he saw available space. He went back to the car and got more bags and she followed, taking the remaining few.

"Is that everything?" he asked, looking at her with his hard, direct gaze.

She looked away. "Yes. That's everything."

"You'll have to show me where everything goes," he said.

"I'll put everything away Ramsey. You've done enough."

"I'll say when enough is enough," he told her.

She glanced at him. Smiled just barely. "The canned food and boxes go here," she said walking over to the pantry, opening it.

"Got it," he said. He took a few bags there and began unpacking them.

She observed him putting cans on the shelf. "I'm surprised you're actually here and talking to me after Friday night."

"Why is that?"

"You know why. The date was horrible."

"It wasn't horrible, Gianna."

"It was because I wasn't comfortable in that setting. I knew I wouldn't be. I told you that."

"Yeah, you did warn me. It's my fault for not listening to you. I'll try my hardest not to make that mistake again." He placed two more cans on the shelf.

"Why were you at Harris Teeter on University City Boulevard when you live in Lake Norman?"

"I was picking up some ranch dressing on the way to my parent's house. They live a little further down Mallard Creek. My mother has this big Sunday dinner once a month and Regal forgot the dressing."

"You're supposed to be at your mother's house right now?"

"Yes."

"Then, go."

"No," Ramsey placed a box of elbow noodles on the shelf.

"Ramsey?"

He turned around to look at her once again watching her shy away from his gaze. "Yes?"

"By all means, please go. I don't want to interfere with your family time."

"It's fine. I already informed Regal that something important came up and, in case you're wondering, *you're* the something important." He finished unpacking then scooped up the plastic bags off of the floor. "Do you save these?"

"Yes. I'll take them." When Gianna reached for the bags, their hands touched. The spark it generated was enough to set her on fire – house and all.

"Thanks."

"You're welcome." Ramsey slid his hands into the pockets of his slacks and looked around, in no hurry to leave. "You have a nice place. It suits you."

"Thanks. Um, can you excuse me for a moment? I'll be right back."

"I'll be here," he said, then flashed a smile at her.

Gianna's stomach quivered when she caught his beautiful smile before walking away to check on Gemma. When she opened the door to Gemma's bedroom, she saw her sleeping soundly. Gianna smiled, left a light kiss on her cheek, then closed the door quietly as she exited.

Returning to the kitchen, she saw Ramsey on his cell phone. Sounded like he was ordering food. After he ended the call, he attached his phone to the belt clip at his waist and said, "Dinner will be here shortly."

"You really don't have to do that," she said, standing by the table, keeping a good distance away from him.

"I know. I want to do it."

"Why?"

"You've been stressed out all day working on unpacking bags. I want to alleviate some of that."

"That's not your job, Ramsey."

"Then whose job is it, Gianna?"

She froze. She hadn't thought about it like that. Probably because she never had that kind of support in her life. Sure, she had Felicity, but Felicity wasn't a man. And Gianna used to dream about what it would be like to fall in love, to have someone who was willing to love you, protect you and be there for you no matter what. Then again, her mother had those same dreams and she never could find a man who was able to do those things for her. Maybe that's why she relied on herself for everything. It didn't work for her mother. Why would it work for her?

Looking at Ramsey, she said, "What I mean is, I don't want you to feel obligated to do anything for me."

"I don't. I do what I do for you out of the goodness of my heart. And, because I like you," he added.

"You like me?"

He flashed a smile. "Yes, Gianna. I like you."

"I don't understand. You were obviously upset when we parted ways Friday night."

He grinned. "How was I *obviously* upset?"

"You asked me if I wanted dessert while I was still eating my spaghetti. You may as well had stood up and shouted, *dinner's over. Get me out of here!*"

He chuckled.

She continued, "And then, you walked me to my car and didn't hug me, kiss me on the cheek or anything. You just opened my car door and closed it."

"You know what, Gianna. If I didn't think you would panic and slap me, I would've hugged you and kissed you on the cheek, but you were already uncomfortable, sweetness, and I didn't want to make matters worse for you. It had nothing to do with me being upset. It had everything to do with me respecting your boundaries."

"Well, even still, you were upset about how the date went."

He narrowed his eyes at her and leaned against the counter, crossing his arms over his chest. "Yes, I was upset—no, more like frustrated. A little."

"Why?"

"Because you wouldn't give me what I wanted. You kept the conversation *generic,* and I needed something deeper from you. That frustrated me. So, now I'm here to get from you what I didn't get Friday night—your heart."

"My—my heart?"

"Yes."

"What does that mean?"

"It means I want to know you—I want to know what matters to you. I want to know why you cry. I want to know about the things, circumstances and situations that stress you out. I want to know why you've never been in love. Why it's so hard for you to accept help when you're the type of woman to go above and beyond for others? I want to know those things. The deeper things."

When the doorbell sounded, he said, "It's probably the take-out. I got it." He walked to the door and gave the driver two twenty-dollar bills then returned to the kitchen with a paper bag.

"Are you ready, Gianna?"

"To eat?"

"Yes, and to give me your heart."

"That's a strange request."

"Once you get to know me, you'll see that it's not so strange. What do you say?"

"Okay. I'll try."

"That's all I can ask of you." He took the food containers from the bag and set one on the table in front of her and the other for himself. "I ordered a plate for Gemma, too."

"She's sleeping right now."

"Do you think I'll get to meet her before I leave?"

"I don't know." Gianna opened her tray and instantly her mouth began to water as she looked at the Stromboli.

"It's pepperoni and sausage," Ramsey told her.

"It looks good. Thank you."

"No problem."

"I'm sure it's not better than your mother's cooking."

"Doesn't come close," he said smiling.

"I feel like I need to personally apologize to

her for ruining your family dinner."

"You didn't ruin dinner."

"I did. You're supposed to be there. You're not because you're here with me."

"No worries. My mother is a very understanding woman but if you insist, I'm sure you'll get the chance to apologize to her one day."

Gianna looked up at him when he made the statement, watching as he sank his teeth into the Stromboli as he took a bite. Did he not hear what he just said? That one day she would get to apologize to his mother which meant she would get to *meet* his mother which, in turn, meant that in his mind, he intended for this 'thing' between them to be long-term.

"Let's talk about your parents—can we start there?" he asked.

Gianna grimaced.

"Let me put your mind at ease. I'm not going anywhere, Gianna."

"Huh?"

"I'm not going anywhere. I'm here. At your disposal. You can use me however you like."

What the—? "You say that so nonchalantly like it's not a big deal. You have a business to run."

"I took a month off."

Her eyebrows raised. "An entire month?"

"Yes. Tell me about your parents?"

Gianna's chewing slowed. She took a moment to finish what was in her mouth then washed it down with a swallow of water.

Ramsey studied her hesitancy. To make her

more comfortable, he said, "I'll tell you about my parents first. My mother's name is Bernadette. Father, Mason. They've been married for forty-two years and are still in love. My mother is a retired schoolteacher. My father was an engineer for a train company."

"What subject did your mother teach?"

"Chemistry."

"Really?" Gianna asked, remembering how complicated chemistry was.

"Yes."

"Cool. They sound lovely."

"They are. They've always been good parents."

"Then, you're lucky. My situation is entirely different—so different, you couldn't relate."

"Maybe not, but I will try to understand. It will help me better understand you."

"Why do you want to understand me?"

"I find you interesting."

Gianna grinned nervously. "I think you're looking at me through filters, but I promise you...there are no enhancements to make me something I'm not. Unfortunately, what you see is what you get."

"Good. That's what I was hoping for. Tell me about your parents."

He was a persistent man. She'd give him that. Glancing up at him, watching him chew his food for a few seconds made her lose her train of thought. Ramsey was one of those men – like *those* men – the type of man women gushed over but could never attain because he was so far out of their reach. And here he was, in arm's-length of her, giving her all of his attention. *Strange*, she thought. She'd had men who were interested – lesser men than him by her own judgment – but never a man like him. She never had a man pay her this much attention, come to the bakery to see her and look at her with such longing in his eyes.

"Gianna?"

"Oh," she said leaving her thoughts behind to pay attention to him. "Um...my parents."

"Yes."

"Well, I don't know who my father is, and I doubt my mom knows."

"Have you inquired about it?"

"Yes. Plenty of times when she was around. All she would say was that he was a black man. Said he was half white, half black, and he didn't care about me."

"She told you that?"

Gianna nodded. "She didn't like him very much. Sometimes, she would sit and reminisce about him and would get upset with me because she said I had his eyes. She used to say, *don't look at me with the eyes of that devil.*"

Ramsey frowned. "Seriously?"

"Yeah, because apparently, I have my father's light brown eyes."

"I happen to think you have the most beautiful eyes I've ever seen. That is, when you let me see them."

She smiled. "Thank you."

"You're welcome." He took a sip of water. "Continue please."

"Oh, um...so she was angry at him, I think,

because he didn't marry her. Over the years, I've watched my mother jump from man to man—to anyone who sold her a dream. She was determined to find a man to make her *whole*, she said. To make all of her dreams a reality. She didn't want to put in the work to fulfill her own goals and ensure her own success. She wanted to find a successful man who had all the things she wanted."

"I see. And where does Gemma fit into all of this?"

"I was almost ten when Gemma was born. I don't know her father either. After mom gave birth to Gemma, I felt like she gave up hope of finding her prince charming since Gemma's dad didn't stick around, either. After that, she was even more promiscuous. Every time I turned around, there was a different man. And she would leave for days at a time. I remember being eleven and changing Gemma's diaper and feeding her. I practically became her caretaker. As a teenager, when it came time for me to go to school, I would take Gemma to my neighbor's house in the mornings and make up a lie about why mom wasn't home. Gosh, at thirteen, I felt like a teen mom. And the crazy thing is, my neighbor knew I was lying, but she never reported the situation to the authorities, thank God, or I don't know where we would be. So, long story *long*, I don't know where my mother is and I don't have a father. Well, I do have one—I just don't know who he is or where he is."

Ramsey nodded, taking this all in. "It

must've been difficult taking care of your sister like that."

"It wasn't easy. I just did what had to be done."

"I see." Ramsey gathered up his trash and got up from the table to walk it over to the garbage.

Gianna watched him walk there. He looked extra tall in her house for some reason and the outfit he wore today – a pair of dark slacks and a short-sleeved white Polo shirt showed off his leanness. His muscles. She could see the corded ropes in his arms as well as the bulge of his biceps underneath the short sleeves. He was the purest form of male she'd ever laid eyes on.

When he turned around, she hurried and looked away.

"Are you done eating?" he asked.

"Yes." She was way too nervous to eat another bite. She did manage to eat a good portion of the Stromboli before her appetite left her.

"Then, do you mind if we sit in the living room for a while?" he asked.

A while...

"Um, okay."

Gianna stood up, closed her takeout container and followed him to the sofa.

He sat on the right side.

She took the left.

"When we talked at the bakery, you said you liked baking," he said.

"I do."

"But it's not your passion," he said. "I want

to know why you opened the bakery if it's not your passion."

"You don't forget anything, do you?" Gianna asked, fumbling with her fingers.

"No, I don't. I'm an architect. I pay excessive attention to detail...like the way you hardly look at me when we talk and how your hands always twitch whenever I'm close to you. Relax."

Easy for you to say. "Okay, well, um...I didn't have time for me when I was growing up. I had to be there for Gemma. So, I didn't go to college. I worked at a bakery full-time after graduating high school while taking classes part-time at a technical school for business administration. It took me four years to get a two-year degree, but I finally got my Associate's degree. Still, I kept working at the bakery. Jobs were hard to come by when I graduated so I got the crazy idea to start my own bakery. I worked, and worked and worked some more until I had enough startup money, well in conjunction with a small business loan. Around the same time, I found out Gemma was sick."

"Sick?"

"Yes. She—" Gianna paused. "She has lung cancer." Gianna swallowed the hurt and forced her way through. With a shaky voice, she continued, "I put the bakery on hold and started doing all kind of cancer research while focusing on her treatment. After the cancer went into remission, I felt like I could finally breathe again, so I moved ahead with opening the bakery and life was good for a little while.

Everything seemed normal. Then the cancer came out of remission four months ago. I tell you that to say this—I love baking, but it stopped becoming something I enjoyed when it became a job that could barely pay for my sister's healthcare. And, I don't do this job for me anymore. It's all for her."

Ramsey thought for a moment, remembering how difficult it was for him to move forward with his business plans after losing Leandra. Switching gears, he asked, "Where is your mother now?"

"Now, like right at this moment?"

"Yes."

Gianna shrugged. "I don't know."

"When did you last see her?"

"A few years ago."

"Years? Does she know Gemma's sick?"

"Yeah. She knows. She just doesn't care."

Ramsey stared at Gianna for a moment. She carried a lot of pain, he realized, and he wanted nothing more than to take that pain away, even if it meant reliving his own heartbreak. "Do you mind if I slide closer to you?"

Gianna's body immediately locked up. "Why can't you just stay over there?"

"Because it's difficult for me to put my arms around you from way over here."

"You want to put your arms around me?"

"Yes. It won't hurt. I promise." He smiled.

"I—I have to check on Gemma. Excuse me," Gianna said standing and hurrying out of the room. She walked to Gemma's bedroom stepped inside and closed the door. With her back pressed against the door, she fought for air while the thought of Ramsey's arms around her made her heart pound out of control. He wanted to put his arms around her, he said. She couldn't let that happen. She'd never been encased in a man's arms before, but then again, she was experiencing many firsts with Ramsey. She'd never had a man in her house. Never had a man help her put away groceries. Never had a man look at her the way Ramsey's eyes seemed to pierce her soul.

"Okay, Gianna," she said to herself heaving, trying to get her breathing under control. All this and the man hadn't laid a hand on her, yet. "You have to find a way to get him to leave." She had no idea how she would do so.

She looked over at Gemma. She was still sleeping soundly.

"Think, Gianna. Think. Think. Think! How can you get him to leave? You could just ask him to. He's a gentleman. Right? He'd leave if you asked nicely. So, do it. Ask him."

She grimaced, wondering if it was normal for a woman to have this much difficulty dealing with a man. She wanted him to stay but her nerves needed him to leave. She smiled nervously and with a spurt of confidence, she left Gemma's bedroom and headed back to the living room where she saw Ramsey sitting in the same spot on the couch.

"Ramsey, I—"

"Come sit here next to me," he interrupted her to say, patting the area of the sofa to his immediate left.

Crap. What now, Gianna?

Slowly, she took steps in his direction then sat dead center of the sofa. He scooted closer, closing the gap between them – his woodsy cologne touching her nose before his left thigh jammed up against her right.

"You've had a long day," he said, his eyes like radar on the side of her face.

Gianna shivered when she felt his warm breath touch her face.

He draped his arm around her and her shiver became a quiver. She was too tense, too uncomfortable to let his arm remain around her. Grabbing a hold of his hand, she moved his arm from around her and said, "I'm sorry. I'm not comfortable with that."

"Why?"

"Because I'm just not."

"Can you try to be because I really want to hold you?"

"Ramsey—"

"Just this once," he said. "If you don't want it to happen again after this time, it won't. Can you make that compromise?"

"Okay."

Ramsey put his arm around her again and this time, he gently pulled her closer to his chest. When she seemed okay with that, he locked his other arm around her and rested his chin on her head.

"This feels strange," Gianna said, pulling in the wonderfully intoxicating smell of his skin.

"Just relax and get used to me," he said in a soft, seductive tone.

Get used to me – the things he had the nerve to say, but Gianna obliged, closed her eyes and did what Ramsey suggested – relaxed. It was in those quiet moments that she could feel and appreciate the warmth of his body heat and bathe in the comfort that only a man could provide a woman. She could enjoy being taken care of for once in her life. She could be content enough to fall asleep right here in his arms.

"Gianna," Ramsey whispered softly.

"Yes?"

"If things in your life were different and you had a normal upbringing, do you think you would've been married by now?"

"No."

He chuckled. "Why not?"

"Because I'd still be weird. That's not a trait men look for in the woman they want to settle down with."

"You're not weird."

"I am. You don't have to be nice, Ramsey. I know what I am."

"You're not weird, Gianna. You're inexperienced. There's a difference."

"Well, whatever the case, the answer to your question is, no."

"Do you want marriage?"

"I thought I did. Now, I'm not sure. I'm not sure about a lot of things, so I just try to take life one day at a time now to see where it takes me."

"There's nothing wrong with that," Ramsey said. After a few silent moments, Ramsey adjusted his position when he felt her lean further into him and release a long, satisfying, humming sound. Had she fallen asleep that quickly?

"Gianna," he whispered.

When he didn't receive a reply, he smiled, satisfied that she was comfortable enough to fall asleep in his arms.

"Rest, sweetness. You deserve to." He rubbed his hand across her soft, silky hair and exhaled deeply feeling just as at peace and comfortable as she was.

"You must be Ramsey."

The voice made him open his eyes to look for its source and that's when he saw her, Gemma, wearing a long, quilted cardigan with a turquoise scarf tied on her head.

"I am. You must be Gemma."

She smiled lazily. "So, she's told you about me, huh?" She coughed.

"A little. Yes."

"She usually doesn't say anything. She doesn't want sympathy from anybody, you know."

"Yeah, I know. Where is Gianna's bedroom?"

"Upstairs. The door at the very end of the hallway."

"Okay. She's asleep, so I'm going to take her up so you and I can talk. Will that be okay?"

"Yeah. Sure."

Ramsey carefully eased Gianna into his arms and effortlessly scooped her up, then headed upstairs. Pushing her bedroom door open with his foot, he walked in and lowered her down on the bed. Then he looked around her room for a piece of cover to spread over her. He smiled. Her room looked pretty and girly. It suited her – pastel pink walls – same color as the walls in the bakery. She had a princess bed with buttercream covers along with the matching color curtains, nightstands and rugs.

In an armchair that sat in a corner of the room near the bed, he saw a plush pink blanket. He took it, spread it over her then strummed his index finger along the side of her soft jawline. "I'll be back, sweetness," he whispered, then quietly left her room, pulling the door closed.

Eagerly, he returned downstairs to find Gemma in the kitchen. She'd just taken a can of soup from the pantry.

"So, that's why Gianna buys so much soup. It's for you."

"Yes. For me. It's food I can easily consume and prepare." Gemma set the can of soup on the counter, then stretched out her small, weak hand to Ramsey for an introductory shake.

Ramsey looked at her hand and stepped closer, opening his arms and embracing her thin frame. With all the care in the world, he palmed the back of her head and brought her close to his chest, the same way he used to embrace his dying fiancée. His eyes watered just slightly before he sucked in a breath, foregoing his pain and past to be present for her. For Gemma.

"I'm sorry you have to go through this. I truly am." He released her.

"You say that like you can relate."

"I can," he said.

Gemma took a bowl from the cupboard.

Ramsey opened the soup for her, poured it in the bowl and placed it in the microwave. "Have a seat, Gemma. I'll bring it to you when it's ready."

"O-kay."

He smiled warmly at her. When the microwave dinged, he removed the bowl.

"The spoons are in the drawer right there in front of the microwave," Gemma told him.

He opened the drawer, took a spoon then placed the bowl on the table in front of her.

He sat down, watched her take a spoonful to her mouth.

She glanced up at him. Smiled. "Gianna said you were handsome. Boy did she hit the nail on the head. Good God, you're gorgeous."

Ramsey chuckled. "Thank you. I see you're not shy like your sister."

"No. We're complete..." Gemma coughed. "Opposites. The closest thing we are to being alike is the fact that our psycho mother wanted our first names to begin with the letter 'G' for some odd reason." Gemma coughed again.

"Are you okay?"

"Yeah. I'm fine. Well, I'm not *fine*. I have cancer, but...you get what I'm trying to say, right?"

He nodded. "Well, my mother isn't psycho, but she named us boys with the letter 'R'. My brother's names are Regal, Romulus and Royal."

"Cool. And different. I like it." Changing the

subject, she said, "Let me ask you something, Ramsey. Why are you interested in my sister?"

"Who says I'm interested?"

"Well, you're here and Gianna told me your date was horrible. She was sure you never wanted to see her again."

"She was wrong, and the date wasn't all that bad."

"It was bad enough for her to think you never wanted to see her again."

"I honestly don't know why she would think that when my every thought has been consumed with her since we met."

Gemma's brows raised. "Your *every* thought?"

"Every last one."

Gemma smiled. "You really like her, don't you?"

"I do."

"Despite all that weird crap she does?"

He grinned. "Yes. Despite of it all."

"Good, because she's going to need you when I'm gone. Gianna is quirky and shy but she has a heart of gold. She uses her time, her energy, her resources—her everything to take care of me. I know I'm dying, but I couldn't go through this without her."

"Don't say that—that you're dying."

"It's true. There's no need in trying to find a glimmer of hope in this situation. I'm dying."

"Haven't you had chemotherapy?"

"Yes, but it's not working this time around."

"Your doctor told you that?"

"No. I have an appointment coming up.

That's what he's going to tell me. I know it's not working because I can feel it. Gianna's going to insist that I try it again. And again and again. Ugh."

"What is she supposed to do, Gemma?"

"Let the inevitable happen."

Ramsey grimaced.

"I see the look on your face, so let me explain," Gemma said. "My sister has taken it upon herself to take care of me. She's doing all this stuff for nothing."

"What stuff?"

"She's emptied her bank account, took out loans, got a second mortgage on the house, maxed out three credit cards and every single dime she makes from that bakery goes toward my health care. I'm a burden to her."

"Don't say that. You're not a burden."

Gemma narrowed her eyes. "How do you know that?"

"Because I've been where your sister is right now. I was in her shoes. I lived it. I know how it feels to—to feel helpless—to wish there was some magic pill that would make everything better, but there isn't. I lost someone close to me...close to my heart, and I know what Gianna is feeling right now. I can feel it without her having to say a word. I knew I was drawn to her for a reason. You are the reason, Gemma."

Gemma pushed the bowl away and pondered what he said for a moment, staring at him as she did so. "So—" she coughed. Cleared her voice. "You think you were attracted to my sister because—"

"As strange as this may sound, my heart attracted her heart which is the reason why I can't leave her alone. I know what she needs. Everything else about her is a bonus."

Gemma smiled.

"I know you feel like you're burdening her, but love carries burdens, sweet girl. If Gianna gave up on you, you'd be in a world of trouble."

"Yeah, but I love her the same way she loves me, Ramsey. I don't want to see her struggle, knowing *I'm* the blame."

"Well, you don't have to worry about her struggling anymore. I'm here. Now, if I heard you correctly, you said you had an appointment tomorrow."

"I have an appointment on Monday."

"Tomorrow is Monday," he told her.

"Oh. Right, then yes. I have a consultation— a follow-up to the chemotherapy from last week."

"What time is the appointment?"

"Nine."

"How do you typically get to your appointments?"

"Gianna takes me."

"She hadn't planned on opening the bakery tomorrow?"

"I guess not."

Ramsey frowned a little while he tried to think of a way to take some of the burden off of Gianna.

"I could try to drive again. I drove myself to the chemotherapy appointment last week."

"No. *I'll* take you before I let you drive. As a

matter of fact, let's do that. I'll drive you."

"No. I appreciate it, but Gianna wanted to be at this consultation with me. She felt bad enough that she couldn't be there last week."

"Right," he said, remembering that he had two appointments already lined up in the morning. Meeting his project managers at the new University City Apartment complex was first on the agenda, then right after, he had an appointment with Wedded Bliss.

"I just hate that the bakery has to close for the day. Has she considered a home health nurse to assist you?"

"We looked into it."

"What happened?"

"Insurance doesn't cover it so it would have to be private pay. They charge close to two-hundred dollars an hour. Can you believe that?" she asked. "And I would need at least four hours, three days a week at a minimum."

Ramsey did the math in his head.

"When your loved one was sick, did you hire a home health nurse, Ramsey?"

"No, but I would have if I could afford it at the time."

She nodded. "I feel so bad for Gianna. When I'm gone, she's going to be the one left suffering. My pain will have ended. I don't want to leave her in pain when I love my sister so much." Tears blurred her vision.

"I told you, Gemma," Ramsey said, reaching across the table to hold Gemma's hands. "That's why I'm here. I'm going to take care of your sister. That I can promise you. Okay?"

Gemma nodded.

Ramsey got up from the table, invited her to stand and closed his arms around her once more. "You don't have to worry about Gianna. Your focus should be on getting better. Let me worry about Gianna."

"Okay."

Releasing her, he asked, "For your appointment tomorrow—is there a copay?"

"Yes."

"How much is it?"

"Fifty dollars."

He removed his wallet and handed her a fifty dollar bill. "Take this. Pay the copay. Okay?"

Gemma, reluctant to accept the money, stood there with her hands by her side.

Ramsey reached for her hand, grasped it, then placed the money in her palm, closing her fingers around it. "Take it."

Gemma knew Gianna probably didn't have the money to pay for it. Last week, she had to borrow the copay from Felicity. "Thank you."

"You're welcome, Gemma."

"I need to lay down now. I'm tired."

Ramsey glanced at his watch. The time was a little after nine, and he had no desire to go home.

"Are you staying?" Gemma asked.

"I want to, but—"

"But what?"

"I would prefer not to sit in here alone. I want to be close to your sister. Do you mind if I sit in her room while she sleeps?"

"Sit?"

"Yes."

"No. I don't mind, but she'll probably freak out if she wakes up and finds you in her room. She's never had a guy up there."

"I won't stay the whole night. Just for a little while."

"Okay."

"Goodnight, Gemma."

"Goodnight, Ramsey."

He watched her walk away until she was no longer in sight. He wanted to know, needed to know everything about her diagnosis. He wanted to know why she had cancer. Was it hereditary? He wanted to know if perhaps there was some treatment that could reverse her diagnosis—experimental or otherwise. He didn't have the resources to save Leandra, but now that money was no object, he could try to save Gemma. A part of him needed to.

After checking the front and back doors, making sure the house was secure, he headed upstairs then walked down the hallway to Gianna's bedroom.

He pushed the door open, noticing her lying in the same position that he'd placed her in an hour ago. She looked exhausted. Her mouth was slightly opened as she slept. Her face looked soft. Peaceful. He liked that. She had no worries while she slept. It was probably the only time she got a reprieve from her hectic, stress-filled life.

He was about to sit in the chair when he noticed a shoe box on her dresser that looked out of place in her neatly organized room. He glanced at her, then walked there, opened it and didn't see shoes. He saw envelopes. Bills. A shoebox full of them. He knew her bills weren't any of his business, but since he felt a deep affinity to her, he decided to make her problems his problems.

He glanced back at the bed to make sure she was still sleeping before taking the first envelope from the box. It was a letter from the property management group that owned the building that housed her bakery, dated a month ago.

From: Queen City Properties, Inc.
To: Gianna Jacobsen
Subject: Lease Past Due

Ms. Jacobsen,

The Boardwalk Bakery, owned and operated by Gianna Jacobsen, is past due on the lease. Please pay this amount in full by July 31st to avoid eviction.

Amount Owed $2,000
Assessed Penalty (5%)
Total: $2100

_____

Ramsey kept going through the pile of envelopes, reading through notices from collection agencies and credit card companies. There was also a notice from the mortgage company:

> From: Pinnacle Funding
> To: Gianna Jacobsen
> Subject: Mortgage Past Due
>
> Ms. Jacobsen,
>
> The mortgage for your property on Arbor Vista Drive has been past due for three consecutive months. We are writing to inform you that unless this amount [$2,937] is received by July 15th, foreclosure proceedings will begin on your home…

————————

Ramsey closed his eyes and sighed, feeling sorry for her. How was it possible that she could still manage to smile at this point in her life? Mounting bills, a dying sister and now her house *and* her business were on the line.

He took out his phone, snapping a photo of the foreclosure notice from the bank as well as the notice from the property management company where she leased the space for the bakery. Then he put everything back inside of the shoe box the same way he'd found it. He walked back over to the chair in the corner and sat there with his elbows resting on his knees, watching her.

She couldn't help but be anxious and nervous. She was buried in debt with no hope of coming out of it—all because she'd given everything to take care of her sister. She'd give anything for Gemma, even if it left her with nothing.

He stood up from the chair and stooped down beside her bed. So close that he was only a breath away from her lips, he whispered, "You don't have to worry anymore, Gianna. I'll take care of you. You're stuck with me now, and I'm never letting go." He leaned even closer until his nose was pressed against her hair. He pulled in a long, deep inhale and released it slowly. Then he stood up and headed downstairs.

Before leaving, he peeped inside Gemma's room to make sure she was okay and after confirming that she was, he quietly exited out of the front door, making sure it was locked.

He sat in his SUV, not attempting to put the car into gear. He just sat there, desiring to go back inside. He didn't want to leave them, but he didn't have much of a choice. Gemma already warned him that Gianna would flip out if she woke up and saw him in her room. Additionally, he had too much on his schedule for tomorrow. He couldn't stay. So, as difficult as it was to do, he slid the gear into reverse and backed out of the driveway.

Chapter 15

"GEMMA, WAKE UP," Gianna said, sitting on her sister's bed at 7:30 in the morning.

Groggy, Gemma cracked her eyes, just barely. "What is it, Gianna?"

"Your appointment is today, sweet girl."

Gemma stretched. "Oh. Right. Appointment." She yawned. "Do we really have to go?"

"Yes, we have to go. I know you're tired, but we can't reschedule this appointment. We gotta go, Gem."

"Okay, okay." Gemma stretched her arms up in the air. "That's what I get staying up late, talking to your boyfriend."

"Huh? You stayed up late last night?" Gianna asked.

Gemma grinned. "You didn't deny that he was your boyfriend." She made kissy faces at Gianna with her lips puckered.

"Who? Ramsey? Oh my gosh! That's right! I fell asleep on the couch," Gianna recalled. "How did I get upstairs?"

"How do you think? I surely didn't take you up there."

"Ramsey?"

"Bingo!" Gemma stood up.

"He—he actually carried me to my

bedroom?"

"Yep. I watched him pick you up as if you were as light as a feather. Then, he came back down and we had a little chat."

Gianna's stomach cinched. "About what?"

"That's between us, but what I *do* know is, he really cares about you."

She couldn't wipe the grin away from her face when she asked, "How do you know that?"

"Stop being nosy, Gianna."

"Nosy?" Gianna said, amused. "You were talking about me. How's that being nosy when I ask you what was discussed?"

"Because it is. Oh, and he gave me the copay for my appointment."

"He did?"

"Sure did."

"Wow. Okay. I'll be sure to thank him."

Pulling a pair of pants from a drawer, Gemma said, "When we were done talking, he went back up to your room. Said he wanted to watch you sleep for a while."

"He did what!"

Gemma smiled lazily. "You should see the look on your face right now." Gemma shook her head. "I don't get you. You have a man as kind and thoughtful not to mention *handsome* as Ramsey and you act like you don't like the attention. Come on. He's perfect."

"Perfect for who?"

"For you, Gianna."

"I—he—ugh...just get ready to go. I'm going to take a shower."

"Yeah, think about Ramsey while you're

rubbing soap all over your body," Gemma said, puckering her lips again.

* * *

Ramsey pulled up at the University City complex site and waited. He glanced at his Rolex. How did he get there before the project managers did? Impatiently, he shook his head. He didn't play when it came down to business.

He watched a black Ford pickup truck pull up with his company's name and logo on the side panel.

Ralph parked and got out of the truck. He walked over to Ramsey's SUV.

Ramsey lowered his window.

"Good morning, Ramsey," Ralph said.

"Good morning. Where's Gilbert, or better yet, where is McFarlane Excavating?"

"Ah…" Ralph took off his hat and surveyed the area, trying to carefully word his response. "Gilbert is on the way and McFarlane promised us they'd be here by 8:30."

Ramsey glanced at his watch. "It's 8:27. If they're not here in three minutes, they're out and I'll have Royal find a replacement."

"With all due respect, Sir, traffic is bad this time of the morning."

"I understand that, but *I'm* here, and I drove from Lake Norman. You're here. If McFarlane really wanted the contract, they would've been here at 8:00, not 8:30. Already, I'm not seeing any commitment from this company."

Ralph sighed. If McFarlane didn't show, he

had a weird feeling that *his* job was on the line. He glanced around again seeing a white, four-door truck pull off the road and onto the entrance of the site.

"Ah, here they come now," Ralph said.

Ramsey glanced at his watch: 8:29 a.m. "Lucky bastards," he mumbled. He turned off the engine and stepped out of the car, walking up to the McFarlane work truck. "You almost got fired," he said boldly, shaking the stocky, white man's hand.

"Sorry about that, Mr. St. Claire. We were running a little behind. This Charlotte traffic ain't no joke, especially on I-85 and I-77."

"Well, our last crew were a no-show, so as you can imagine, I'm pretty ticked about it."

"Yes, Sir. I understand completely."

"Can you and your team do this work?" Ramsey asked, his eyes roaming the site as he did so.

"Yes, Sir. We have the manpower and the tools to get this taken care."

"What timeframe are we looking at?"

The man looked around, surveying the area and said, "Give us two to three weeks."

"I like the sound of two weeks better," Ramsey told him.

"Then two weeks it is."

"Alright. Two weeks," Ramsey said. I haven't worked with you before, but just an FYI...I'm very strict with my deadlines and the due date of this project will be noted on the contract. It is my hope and expectation that you don't run past the due date—but in the event you do, the penalty is two-thousand dollars per day that will come straight out of your pay."

"Shrew. Then we'll definitely have this wrapped up for you, Sir," the man said, chuckling while wiping a thin layer of sweat from his forehead.

Ramsey didn't find any humor in the situation. "Good." He looked at Ralph and placed his hand on his shoulder. "Ralph, here, is the project manager for the site."

"Yes. I spoke with him on the phone last week," the man acknowledged.

"Also, Gilbert, whose on the way, will be assisting with the project as well. Any questions?"

"No, sir."

"Then I'll leave you to it." Ramsey turned to walk away when Ralph said, "Hey, Ramsey."

"What's up?" Ramsey asked.

Ralph fell into stride beside him. "Are you serious about docking them two grand a day if they're late?"

"I am. Why wouldn't I be?"

"Because that's not the rate we usually charge. It's—"

"A thousand per day. I know that. I own this company, Ralph. Do you really think I don't know what the rate is? I do. One thousand...but *this* time, and for *this* job, it's two grand. We already got screwed over once. I'm not going to let it happen again."

"Yes, Sir."

"I'll have my cell phone if you need to reach me. For trivial matters, call Regal or Royal."

"Got it, and Ramsey."

"Yes?" Ramsey asked short of reaching for the door handle of his car.

"We'll handle it, okay. Take a load off, man. Enjoy yourself."

Ramsey gave a single nod then turned away without saying a word more. He got in the Range, pressed the phone button on his steering wheel.

"Please say a command," the voice program prompted.

"Call Cupcake."

"Calling Cupcake," the voice command said.

Ramsey waited, listening to the rings, his heart beating faster than normal as he waited for Gianna to answer. When she didn't pick up, his trepidation worsened. Why wasn't she answering her phone? He knew she was taking Gemma to the hospital. Could she not answer the phone currently? Were they already at the doctor's office? In a patient room? Was everything okay with Gemma – well okay as it could be? It ailed him that he didn't know where that office was. Otherwise, he would've pulled up to talk to her in person and see how Gemma was doing.

Deciding to go ahead with his plans for the day, he drove to South Park, found a parking stall and headed into the building where he would meet with Felicity James. With a folder in hand, he was prepared this time, but he was sure she wasn't going to be prepared for what he had in store for her.

The same receptionist escorted him back to

Felicity's office and he walked in, watching Felicity hold up her index finger. She looked busy, he thought, as busy as the purple and black striped dress she had on and wondered why the receptionist didn't have him sit in the waiting area. Since he was already there, he took a seat and studied Felicity in more detail. She looked like one of those businesswomen who could out talk anyone if they got in her way. The kind of woman who didn't take no for an answer. That's why she agreed to let him look on the database. She didn't think he was capable of finding the right woman for himself. Boy did he have news for her.

Finally hanging up the phone, she took off her headset and placed it on her desk. "Mr. St. Claire...didn't think you were going to show your face today."

Ramsey shot a challenging stare her way. "Why would you think that?"

"Well, you were pretty heated during our last meeting."

"Heated?" He smirked. "You thought *that* was heated?" He lounged back in the chair watching her eyes narrow.

"So, you got a folder. You must've found your *perfect* woman," Felicity made herself say. This was her business, yes, and she'd come up with the concept but for the life of her...some of these guys coming in should've already been snatched up in her opinion. Ramsey was one of those guys. It made her wonder what was wrong with him. Could he not keep a woman happy? Or was he really that peculiar about his type of woman?

Sitting straight up, Ramsey said, "Yes. I did. She's exactly what I want, and I want you to make it happen."

"Okay. May I have a look?"

"Certainly." He leaned forward to place the folder on her desk.

Felicity took it, opened it up and her mouth nearly hit the floor. She frowned, looked up at him and said, "Um...I think there's some mistake."

"No. There's no mistake."

A small grin escaped her mouth. "Okay, um, Gianna Jacobsen is my best friend and her profile wasn't even active on Wedded Bliss' system."

"Oh, it was active. How was I able to retrieve it if it wasn't active?"

"Okay, what I'm trying to tell you is, she's not one of our women. She only entered her information as a favor to me for system testing. She's not looking for a husband and—"

"She's the one I want?"

"She doesn't even have a profile picture listed."

He shrugged. "So what? I told you looks weren't important to me although I have a feeling she's as beautiful as those words make her sound." He nibbled on his bottom lip.

"Okay is this a joke? You're playing me, right? You somehow found out that Gianna was my best friend, and this is how you're getting back at me for our little disagreement the last time we spoke."

"No, not at all. I don't have a personal vendetta against you. I simply want Gianna Jacobsen. Can you make it happen?"

Felicity was beside herself. She was convinced by the smirk on his face that he was playing her. "Do you know Gianna?" she decided to ask.

"I do, no pun intended." He smiled.

"Care to tell me how?" Felicity asked, her eyebrows raised.

"I took her on a date."

Felicity scrunched up her face. "Huh?"

"I took her on a date. We went out."

Then it dawned on her. "Wait—are you the Luce guy?"

He smiled showing his flawless, white teeth. "She told you about that, huh?"

"Oh my God! *You're* the guy?"

"If by *the guy*, you mean the one who took her on a date to Luce and the one who spent the night with her last night, then yes. I'm *the* guy, and she's *my* girl...at least I want her to be. I want you to make it happen. Draw up the papers. Let's get this thing rolling."

"Uh...um...I can't do that, Mr. St. Claire."

"Yes, you can. That's what you do around here, correct? You make marriages."

"Yes, but besides the fact that Gianna's profile wasn't supposed to be active, I know for a fact that she doesn't want marriage."

"And how do you know that?"

"She's my best friend. I know everything there is to know about her."

"So, tell me if you think she and I would be

good together."

"Absolutely not. You're too...um...what's the word...alpha-like. Your personality is too dominant for Gianna."

"No, it's not."

"Yes, it is," she said.

"Ask her."

"I don't have to ask her. I already know."

"Then you tell me, Ms. James. What kind of man does Gianna like?"

Felicity shrugged. "She doesn't date, so I don't know."

"She doesn't date," Ramsey said matter of factly. "Why's that?"

"Because she doesn't," Felicity said, not wanting to tell him too much.

"Because of Gemma?"

Felicity frowned. *He knows about Gemma, too?*

"I met Gemma last night," he told her. "We had a good little chat about Gianna and how she's put her life on hold to take care of her. I admire that in her. It takes a lot of courage, endurance and suffering, I might add, to do what Gianna is doing for Gemma. That's why I want her. I know what she's going through and I want to be there to help her. You're her best friend. I know you've helped her financially and otherwise, haven't you?"

Frowning, Felicity said, "Uh...yes, but—"

"Now, I want to take over. I know what she needs. I know what her sister needs. I need *you* to convince *her* that she needs me. I need you to have her sign a marriage agreement and I want it done this week. First, I want to spend a couple of more days with her, so how about you present this to her on Friday?"

"Uh...um...yeah...that's not going to work. Sorry."

"Why not?"

"I know this space, Mr. St. Claire. This is what I do. I know people and I know how well they mesh. This – you and Gianna – *will* not work."

"Have you ever been in love, Ms. James?"

"Maybe, but we're not talking about me."

"Right, we're talking about me. I know what I want. I want her. I'm the client. I paid you for this service. I want what I want."

"Are you implying that you *love* Gianna?"

He smiled. "I haven't loved a woman in a very long time. That's not what I'm saying."

"You're the one who brought up the subject of love," Felicity reminded him. "Not me."

"You're right. I brought it up because you seem incredibly uptight for a matchmaker."

"Excuse me?" she asked, arching a brow.

"I would expect a matchmaker to have been in love at least once or twice. Maybe even currently. It should be a prerequisite for your line of work."

Felicity rolled her eyes. She had been in love before, but unfortunately the guy she was with wasn't in love with her.

"But love," Ramsey continued. "I've lost the ability to love. I'm on a fifteen-year loveless streak. Does that answer your question?"

"Yes, it does...yet another reason why a

marriage between you and Gianna wouldn't work. I don't want you to hurt my friend, Ramsey."

"I wouldn't dare."

"She deserves a man who can actually love her. Your friend needs me."

"That's why you're attracted to her? Because you *think* she needs you."

"I don't *think* it. I *know* it, and yes, it is part of my attraction to her. I'll admit, she's a pretty woman. She's beautiful, even when she has flour in her hair or on her nose. But, as I stated to you before when we had the very first consultation, Felicity, I'm attracted to hearts. Her heart needs mine."

"Okay. I get it. You have this strange *calling* to help her. That doesn't mean you have to marry her."

"Yes, it does."

"Why?"

"Because no one else can have her."

"So, let me get this straight. You want to help her, you'll never love her but you don't want anyone else to love her either?"

Ignoring her, Ramsey said, "She's mine, Felicity. Friday, I want you to talk to her and do not mention anything to her about this before Friday. As your client, I'm expecting that you will fully comply with your own privacy and confidentiality clause. Am I right, or do I need to put my attorney on notice?"

"You don't have to threaten me with your attorney. I always abide by my privacy policy."

"Good," he said standing."

"Wait," Felicity said. "How am I going to get her to sign?"

"Tell her everything I'm willing to do for her."

"And what are those things? Enlighten me."

"I will get her sister the highest form of care possible, pay every outstanding hospital bill she has, prevent her home from going into foreclosure, pay off her car, pay the lease on the bakery for the next ten years and whatever else she needs. I'll do it." Ramsey smiled. He'd planned on doing all those things regardless of whether Gianna signed the papers.

"Most likely, she won't go for it," Felicity said. "She'd struggle until she dies before she would have you blackmail her with money."

Ramsey frowned. "Blackmail? This isn't blackmail. I'm helping her."

"If you were sincere in your efforts, you would help her without requiring her to sign over any documents to be your wife."

"I'm sorry. I don't understand what your problem is. This is what you do for a living. Now that it's someone you're close with, you want to hit the brakes. I want Gianna. I told you I won't hurt her."

"And how do I know that? I don't know you. Gianna is my friend, and I would give her the money myself if I could afford to. But this business isn't exactly taking off. If it was, I'd give her all the money she needs to take care of her sister. She's struggling, Mr. St. Claire. For as long as I've known her, she's struggled." Felicity blinked back tears.

Ramsey sat down again, crossed his legs and decided to level with Felicity since she was obviously upset and loved Gianna dearly. "Okay. Listen. I know what Gianna's going through. I know how it feels to lose someone close to me. I think that's what drew me to her. I could sense she was going through something similar, and I was right. I don't love her. I haven't known her long enough to love her. I don't even know if I'm capable of loving anyone after what I've been through. But I am capable of lending a helping hand. I signed up for your service because I wanted companionship. I wanted someone to come along with me on business trips. I wanted to have someone to introduce to my clients. To my family. When I met Gianna, I knew that someone was her. I need to go through this process to find out why. I give you my word that I will not hurt her."

Felicity nodded. "Okay."

Ramsey was about to stand up again but didn't move when he heard Felicity say, "She's shy."

"I've spent enough time with her to know that."

"She doesn't have experience with men, especially men like you."

"I know that, too."

"She has bad nerves. I think being on edge all the time about Gemma did that to her, and I actually believe she's going to have a breakdown when Gemma...when Gemma dies. When Gemma was first diagnosed, Gianna had a mini-stroke. Did you know that?"

203

"No."

"She can't handle much more stress, Mr. St. Claire."

"I know. I'm here to make her life easier, not stress her out. I promise you...I won't hurt her." He placed a hand over his heart and said, "I give you my word."

"I'm going to hold you to that."

~ ~ * ~ ~

Will Gianna sign the agreement? Is there any way Gemma's health can improve? And what about Ramsey? Will taking on the responsibility of helping Gianna interfere with his work at St. Claire Architects?

Look for part two in May! It'll be worth the wait and even SWEETER. In the meantime, please take a moment to leave a review on Amazon.

Also by Tina Martin:

The Blackstone Family Series
*All books in this series are standalone novels and are full, complete stories. Read them in any order.

Evenings With Bryson
Leaving Barringer
Forever Us: Barringer and Calista Blackstone (A short story follow-up to *Leaving Barringer*. You must read *Leaving Barringer* before reading this short story)
The Things Everson Lost

A Lennox in Love Series
*All books in this series are standalone novellas and are full, complete stories. Read them in any order.

Claiming You
Making You My Business
Wishing That I Was Yours
Caught in the Storm with a Lennox (A Short Story Prequel to Claiming You)

Mine By Default Mini-Series:
*This is a continuation series that must be read in order.

Been In Love With You, Book 1
When Hearts Cry, Book 2
You Belong To Me, Book 3
When I Call You Mine, Book 4
Who Do You Love?, Book 5
Forever Mine, Book 6

The Champion Brothers Series:
*All books in this series are standalone novels and are full, complete stories. Read them in any order.

His Paradise Wife
When A Champion Wants You
The Best Thing He Never Knew He Needed
Wives And Champions

The Way Champions Love

The Accidental Series:
*This is a continuation series that must be read in order.

Accidental Deception, Book 1
Accidental Heartbreak, Book 2
Accidental Lovers, Book 3
What Donovan Wants, Book 4

Dying To Love Her Series:
*This is a continuation series that must be read in order.

Dying To Love Her
Dying To Love Her 2
Dying To Love Her 3

The Alexander Series:
*Books 1-5 must be read in order. Book 6 and the spinoff book, Different Tastes, can be read in any order as a standalone.

The Millionaire's Arranged Marriage, Book 1
Watch Me Take Your Girl, Book 2
Her Premarital Ex, Book 3
The Object of His Obsession, Book 4
Dilvan's Redemption, Book 5
His Charity Challenge, Book 6 (Heshan Alexander and Charity Eason)
Different Tastes (An Alexander Spin-off novel. Tamera Alexander's Story)

Non-Series Titles:
*Individual standalone books that are not part of a series.
Secrets On Lake Drive
Can't Just Be His Friend
All Falls Down
Just Like New to the Next Man
Falling Again
Vacation Interrupted

The Crush
Wasn't Supposed To Love Her
What Wifey Wants

ABOUT THE AUTHOR

TINA MARTIN is the author of forty-five romance titles and has been writing full-time since quitting her corporate job in 2013. Readers praise Tina for her strong heroes, sweet heroines and beautifully crafted stories. When she's not writing, Tina enjoys watching movies, traveling, cooking and spending time with her family. She currently resides, in Charlotte, North Carolina with her husband and two young children.

You can email Tina at tinamartinbooks@gmail.com or visit her website for more information at www.tinamartin.net.

69365989R00127

Made in the USA
Columbia, SC
19 April 2017